Brok

Part Seven

Chris Wooding

Cover and illustrations by Steve Kyte

SCHOLASTIC

CHRISTIAN BROTHERS,
PRIMARY SCHOOL,
DRIMNAGH CASTLE,
DUBLIN 12.

Check out the

Broken Sky

website

www.homestead.com/gar_jenna

Scholastic Children's Books,
Commonwealth House, 1-19 New Oxford Street,
London WC1A 1NU, UK
a division of Scholastic Ltd
London ~ New York ~ Toronto ~ Sydney ~ Auckland
Mexico City ~ New Delhi ~ Hong Kong

First published in the UK by Scholastic Ltd, 2000

Text copyright © Chris Wooding, 2000
Illustrations copyright © Steve Kyte, 2000

Lyrics taken from *Knuckle Hungry* are reproduced by kind
permission of Planes Mistaken For Stars

ISBN 0 439 01493 X

Typeset by M Rules
Printed by The Bath Press, Bath

10 9 8 7 6 5 4 3 2 1

All rights reserved

The rights of Chris Wooding and Steve Kyte to be identified as the author and illus-
trator respectively of this work have been asserted by them in accordance with the
Copyright, Designs and Patents Act, 1988.

This book is sold subject to the condition that it shall not, by way of trade or
otherwise, be lent, resold, hired out, or otherwise circulated without the publisher's
prior consent in any form of binding or cover other than that in which it is
published and without a similar condition, including this condition, being imposed
upon the subsequent purchaser.

"What you build, what you've built means nothing
Weighed against what you've left behind"

Planes Mistaken For Stars,
Knuckle Hungry

Broken Sky

QUAIN

JIKKIO

JEDDA & LI'AIN

TASKMASTER

CHIRO

Walkinstown Branch Tel. 4558

1

The Girl who Lived in Solitude

Onward, ever onward. Deep beneath the desert, it was all she knew.

Mi'atte pushed the heavy mine cart along the greased rails that ran down the curving tunnel. On either side of her, workers chipped at the red-brown rock with pickaxes, widening the passageway, bathed in the dull orange light of the glowstones that hung in metal cradles from the roof. Sweat streaked their backs, a combination of exertion and the stifling, inescapable heat. The cruel sun was high in the sky outside, and its warmth penetrated even this far underground, carried by the air that circulated through the tunnels from above.

She averted her eyes as she pushed her load past a pair of Taskmasters, who stood with their arms crossed on either side of the rails. Their dark eyes regarded her menacingly; she could feel them, without daring to look. Her shoulders tightened as she walked between them, fearing that they should speak to her; but they let her pass in peace. Heartened, she redoubled her efforts, her weight applied to shoving the cart full of rocks along the level ground towards the dump. Better not relax until she got there; if she took a rest, the ache in her muscles would become cramp and she would be unable to finish the job. Just this last load, and then she was done. . .

It was a long haul to the dump, and she had been through a strenuous shift, but she was up to it. Months of work had hardened her until her endurance seemed near-inexhaustible. At least the rails were nice and slick; in the deeper reaches of the subterranean network in which she lived, nobody ever bothered to grease them, and it would have taken two strong men to push her cart.

She emerged from the passageway into one of the larger chambers, an enormous cave with a multitude of exits. Great tiers of rock humped up to her left, studded with tunnels and lined with support beams. Pulleys squeaked and baskets full of rocks moved up and down; carts rattled along rails on the higher tiers, mirroring her own efforts; and all around was the constant tap and scrape of the workers as they dug at the walls, wearing away at the desert bedrock to obtain the prizes deep within. Clear spirit-stones: the raw material which later became altered in the hands of the Deliverers to grant Dominion-folk their powers.

It was a hard life, but it was the only life she had.

At the dump, she rolled the mine cart on to the tipping platform, locked its wheels into the metal ruts and stood back to let the operator do his job. The platform slowly tilted until the car stood at a right angle, the rocks jumbling out to spill on to the immense heap below. She watched them fall with a faraway look in her eyes. The operator, a swarthy man with a shaven head, glanced at her and then away, a fleeting expression of sorrow on his face. Even an old hand like him felt a stab of remorse at the sight of a girl so young – somewhere between fifteen and twenty winters – working down in the mines. And it was not even as if she had some crime to pay off, like most of them did. She had been bought by the Overseer for the price of a few coins and a meal. She was a slave.

Mi'atte didn't talk much, but she thought a lot. It unnerved her fellow workers, who had long learned that the best way to make life under the earth bearable was to do the opposite. Many times they would find her, drifting with that odd look on her face, her pupils focused on the middle distance as if seeing something that only she could see. At first, the Taskmasters would beat her if they caught her; but soon they learned that she would snap out of it if left alone, and they shared a measure of the other workers' sympathy with her situation. She was no criminal. She had never committed an offence against Macaan, not even one of the trumped-up charges that had condemned many of the people here to a life of toil. She just had no past, and that made her vulnerable. She had been cruelly used. Even the Taskmasters were only human.

The tipping complete, Mi'atte pushed the cart

to a side-buffer and left it there in a queue of two others. She smoothed her hands across her face, smudging streaks of dirt and sweat across her skin, and ruffled the short, tangled thatch of her hair. Rolling her tired shoulders in their sockets, she made her way from the dump up to the cells. People glanced at her as she passed, but nobody hailed her with the friendly camaraderie that even the newest convict usually received. They had long learned that they would be met with indifference from her, the loner, the girl who lived in solitude in a place where companionship was the only pleasure left.

Her cell was the same as a thousand others. It was a small, roughly carved cave with a straw-lined sleeping pallet, lit by a single glowstone that emitted the omnipresent orange-hued light. A tiny, battered chest held spare underclothes, vests and leggings, for the mines could get terrifically cold when it was night-time on the surface.

And resting in the corner was her prize; a sheet of silvery metal, a reflector stolen from the upper levels, where the chambers were so large that glowstones alone could not light them without aid. These thin slabs were arranged along the walls so that they bounced and magnified the meagre illumination provided by the clustered stones and spread it around the cavern. It was cheaper than giving glowstones to each worker.

Mi'atte had taken one. She had resisted the terrible compulsion for many shifts before it became unbearable, and finally she had to give in. Something inside her, something from the void that was her past, had drawn her to it, made her look at herself for the first time.

This is me, she had thought, and suddenly she had to have it. But it was not only that she was fascinated with the girl that looked back at her from within the shiny frame of the reflector, the unfamiliar face that peered at her curiously. It was the reflector itself, something about it . . . something about *mirrors* . . . a dark and frightening feeling that at once repelled and intrigued her. And until she knew why, she could not leave it alone.

It had been a risk. She would have been badly beaten, even killed, if she had been caught. But she did it anyway. For this was by far the strongest cry from the person she had once been, the person *before*, and every moment of her life was consumed with the need to know who that person was. The Taskmasters never checked the cells; in the harsh world of the mines, it was the unwritten law that a convict's territory was his own. There were other mines, said the gossips, further north (wherever *north* was) that had no such rule. But to the desert-folk of the Dominions, a person's territory was sacred, and the Overseer understood that. Even as criminals, they were given their space.

She stood now in front of the reflector and looked at herself. Beneath the grime and dried sweat there was a face that had been described as pretty by the slaver who sold her. She did not know. There was little beauty down here in the mines with which to draw a comparison. But gazing into her own eyes, she felt the familiar tug of memory, as of her past scratching at a distant door, begging to be let in. Somewhere, there was the key to that door. Somewhere.

It was then that she noticed what was lying on the floor by the reflector.

A tiny frown furrowed her brow. She hesitated, then knelt down and picked up the item that had been left for her. A strange thing: three heavy iron balls, each with a single bladed fin jutting out from its smooth surface, attached by a three-way chain.

I should know this, she thought. *It should mean something.* But even though she turned it in her hands for a long time, examining it from every angle, the strong sensations that it evoked refused to coalesce into a clear recollection. Eventually, frustrated, she went over to her chest and opened it. From within, beneath the folds of the heavy woollen night-clothes, she took out two other items and laid them on the floor next to the new arrival in the shape of a triangle.

A tiny, greyish stone, a flat diamond on the end of a thin chain. A much bigger pendant, made of silver, depicting a blazing sun with a hollow centre, and a symbol that she did not recognize within it. And now this strange contraption, possibly a weapon, tinted orange in the shadowy light of the glowstone.

Sitting on the edge of her pallet, she looked

from one to the other, seeking connections, trying to understand. It was the third time in ten shifts that she had found an unfamiliar object in her room. How were they getting there? It would certainly be an easy matter for someone to slip in and leave them. The cells had no locks on – the Overseer would not concede *that* much to his prisoners – and she worked regular shifts, so it would be a simple matter to predict when she would be away. But why?

Someone's trying to tell me something, she thought. *Something about my past.*

Next shift, she was in the light caverns. Prisoners were rotated on the duty roster so that they got to work in the upper caverns at least once every five shifts, unless they were being punished. Here, there were great rents in the rock ceiling that arched high overhead, and vast slices of dazzling sunlight slanted diagonally down into the cavern, gradually travelling across the floor in perfect synchronicity as the day wore on.

The cavern was bowl-shaped, with wide rock tiers descending from the edges towards the pit of the centre. Ladders rested against the walls, providing the means to move up and down levels, and elsewhere were the small cranes, winches, platforms and pulleys that formed the framework of the mining operation.

Mi'atte worked on one of the mid-level tiers. They did not allow the women to perform the heavy pickaxe work, but here a small cluster of spirit-stones had been discovered and they needed someone with a finer touch to mine them out without damaging them. Mi'atte was known as being particularly good at that kind of work. She just seemed to have a feel for the stone.

Now she stood in the centre of a sunbeam, chipping delicately at the reddish, crumbly rock surrounding the small, colourless ovals of the spirit-stones. The hot light drenched her from above and behind, surrounding her in swirling motes of dust, her body casting long lances of shadow as she worked. The heat was bordering on painful, but she relished it. The sun was life. She had seen what happened to those who had been deprived of the light caverns for months, those who had spent dozens of shifts in the deeper tunnels because they had broken mine regulations. She tried not to think about what might have happened to her if she had been caught stealing the reflector.

Shading her eyes, she paused from her work and looked up at the blinding slash in the ceiling that was the source of her sunbeam, and for a moment experienced a jolt of *déjà vu*. That was what she had seen, the first moment she opened her eyes. The sun, impossibly bright above her. And agony. Absently, she tugged at her Damper Collar, rubbing at the itch that the pooling sweat had caused. All the workers with spirit-stones were fitted with Damper Collars. The single white Damper stone sunk into the thin band of metal set up a negation field around them, making their other stones useless. Couldn't have them using their powers to break out.

"Mi'atte!" said a scrawny man with perhaps forty winters behind him who was hacking at the rock near by. She turned to him, and for a moment she was frozen in the fierce light, one side of her face a dazzling white and the other an impenetrable black, half angel and half demon.

And then the moment passed, and the man motioned at the pair of Taskmasters who stood close by. She nodded to her workmate in thanks for his warning, and returned to her industry, keeping a wary eye on her captors.

The Taskmasters walked between them always, the fists of the faceless Overseer who ran the mines for King Macaan. They were the heretics, those desert-people who had allowed their bodies to be corrupted by spirit-stones in the way that the northern Dominion-folk did. Ex-prisoners who had made a deal in exchange for freedom from slavery. Macaan granted them their stones to give them power over their fellow man, and in return they became his jailors. They were still trapped for ever in the mines, but now they were the masters. They went barechested in the sweltering heat, wearing only boots and hardwearing brown trousers. Their dark-skinned bodies were well muscled, the curving swirl that was the mark of the Taskmasters tattooed across their pectorals. Most had their hair matted into dreadlocks in the fashion of the desert nomads, but all of them wore black leather masks across the lower half of their face, beneath their eyes. Those masks irritated Mi'atte. They reminded her of something, some other mask, that she had seen once . . . where there was another mine, a long time ago. . .

She looked away. The memory slipped out of her grasp like smoke.

It was an easy shift. She had the sunlight, and she took her time carving out the spirit-stones so as not to be moved on to a harder job. When it was over, she made her way to the meal hall, where she ate alone. The meal was a stew of thick chunks of meat with heavy root vegetables swimming around them. The prisoners in the mine were fed and cared for well; it made them live longer, work harder and be less inclined to revolt. More productive in the long run.

She returned to her cell after that, intending to take a nap before going to the hot underground spring to bathe. Cleanliness prevented disease, said the Overseer, and in this isolated underground community with its hot atmosphere, a virus could quickly become an epidemic. But as she entered, shutting the thin wooden door behind her on its slightly crooked hinges, she noticed with mild surprise that something new had been left for her, in the shadows where the glowstone's light was faint. Curious as to this new artifact, she went over to it and picked it up, holding it in front of her.

It hit her with an almost physical force, like some huge battering ram cannoning into her. Oh, none of the sensations had ever been this *strong*, nothing had been like this . . . this. . .

Hate.

And somewhere inside her, a long-dormant flame flickered back to life, a flame that burned cold. She looked at the mask in her hands, the oval of silver fashioned into a face that was hideously distended in a scream.

Death, it said to her. *Death*.

For a long time, she stared at it, looking into its empty eyes. Then her hands fell slack at her sides, and it dropped from numb fingers to clatter on the stone floor. She turned to the reflector that was propped up in the corner and gazed at the girl who stood there. She was tall for a girl, almost lanky; and beneath the dirt, she *was* pretty, with beautiful forest-green eyes and hair a deep red. It was short and tangled now, but it hadn't always been that way.

She watched her lips as she mouthed her name. Not the name the slavers had given to her, but her *real* name.

Kia.

It was then that she noticed the keys lying on the straw of her pallet.

2

Between Dusk and Dawn

In the depths of the mines, the dim orange light never waxed and waned with the passing of day and night above. Only the temperature indicated the cycle of sun and moon, for the desert was bitterly cold between dusk and dawn, and the mines took on a harsh chill. The majority of the shifts were carried out during the two-thirds of the day when the tunnels ranged between pleasantly warm and swelteringly hot; working at night was usually either given as punishment detail or because some kind of quota had to be met, and then usually only in the deepest sections. Around the upper levels, there was a curfew. Prisoners were allowed to move about only within their cell corridors; straying outside brought severe retribution.

Mi'atte's cell was vacant. Her chest was closed. Inside it was the spirit-mask and the silver pendant. She had taken only the odd triple-chained weapon and the small diamond-shaped stone that she wore around her neck; the rest she had left behind. She had the impression that they did not belong to her, and it made her uncomfortable to take them. The stone was definitely hers, and the weapon . . . well, she needed to defend herself, and somehow, it felt right to take it. The reflector remained, mirroring the empty room. The Damper Collar lay unlatched and buried beneath the straw of her sleeping-pallet.

She crept through the corridors, wrapped tight in several layers of brown and grey fur, her breath pluming the air. Even through the thick insulation, the cold caused her leg and wrist to ache, an insistent stiffness that reminded her of the broken bones with which she had awoken, with the blinding sun in her eyes. The first clear moment that she could remember.

Kia. Was that her name? Yes, yes it *had* to be. It felt right. And the mask. . . The hatred she felt for the mask told her of some purpose, some reason, something she had to do. And whatever that thing was, she was quite sure it was not down here in the mines. Her anonymous helper had told her that much, by giving her the ring of keys that had unlocked her Damper Collar. She had used the other keys on several doors already, moving with as much stealth as she could manage through the mines. She had had no idea how well-patrolled these areas were, but she soon realized that the Taskmasters were satisfied with the security that the locked doors provided, and were not willing to endure the cold to walk the empty tunnels.

She had almost managed to lull herself into this false sense of confidence when she heard the approaching rumble of the Crawler.

Swearing under her breath, she looked frantically left and right. She was in a long and narrow tunnel, with only a metal door a little way ahead offering any place to hide. Quickly, she hurried over and tried it, the steam of her exhalations coming more rapidly now. It was locked. She glanced either way up the passage. There was no way to tell how far it went before it branched off, and she had not come across any side-tunnels recently. And the noise was getting louder frighteningly fast.

The Crawlers. Everyone in the mines knew about the Crawlers. They were the grinding, roaring machines that carved out the rough tunnels and caverns to allow the miners to get into the seams of spirit-stones, deep in the earth. Shaped like a squat cylinder lying on its side, they had four sets of thick caterpillar tracks set at right-angles around its body which gripped the floor, walls and ceiling of the tunnels they made. Their front end was a mass of whirling drill bits, bores and screws.

It wasn't the Taskmasters who patrolled the tunnels at night. It was the Crawlers.

She fumbled with the keys, but her hands were numb from the cold and the chill metal ring made it worse. The volume of the dull, menacing rumble ascended rapidly as she tried one key, then another, working her way feverishly through the unmarked array.

No good, no good, she thought, biting her lip in frustration as she chose wrongly again and again. In her agitation, she had lost track of which ones she had tried and which she hadn't; they all looked near-identical. Once more, she glanced up the corridor, scared now, overwhelmed by the thunder that swelled around her.

There it was. Appearing from around the curve of the tunnel, its front end whirring with oily blades and drills, filling up the whole passageway with its metal bulk. It ground inexorably on towards her, and she let out a frightened yelp as she scrabbled at the keys again, finding another dud, and another, and all the time it was getting closer. . . *Too late!*

She shrieked and pressed herself against the wall of the tunnel, a futile and instinctive attempt to avoid the iron monster that bore down on her; and then she was falling, the rock giving way behind, and she tripped backwards and fell through the fissure that had opened. The bellowing Crawler rumbled by inches from her feet, on the other side of the wall, filling the wound in the rock for a few moments and then disappearing, its anger beginning to fade.

Kia lay on her back where she had landed, panting. It took her a short time to piece together what had happened, and why she was not now dead.

The wall . . . it opened behind me. I did that.

Her stones. Instinct had made her use her stones. And now she remembered, now she sensed how to use them again, and she could not believe that she had forgotten. It was as natural to her as the process of her heart beating, or her lungs filling and emptying.

She stood up and looked around the storeroom that she had ended up in. After spending a little time calming herself from her encounter with the Crawler, she tried a few experimental efforts with her stones. Raising a four-foot-high golem and moving it around. Drawing patterns in raised lines on the rock roof.

Kia smiled to herself. Though she remembered nothing specific before the time when she had awoken to the blazing sun, she did remember skills that were either instinctive or had been ingrained after much practice. When they had found her, she had been speaking the northern Dominion dialect. She had not forgotten how to walk and run and fight. And though she was a little rusty after a year of wearing a Damper Collar, she had not forgotten how to wield her stones.

She pulled the strange, three-chained weapon from her belt and hefted it in her hand.

Time to get out of here, she thought.

She closed her eyes, and sent herself out into the rock. Meshing with the soil, resonating through the ground, she probed and swept and studied, using infinitesimal vibrations to plot the extent of the mines. Wherever there was nothing, where there was only air where there should have been the ageless bulk of stone, there she knew there was a tunnel. Slowly, carefully, she built up a mental map, choosing a route to the surface and memorizing it, holding it in her head while she drew back the invisible power that pulsed from her: the Flow, the lifeblood of the planet that she channelled through her stones, moulding it to her desire.

Her eyes snapped open.

"Got it," she said to herself, and then she was away.

It was an easy matter to avoid the Crawlers now that she had the use of her stones back. They set up vibrations that could be felt a great distance away by someone like her; and they were not difficult to evade, now she had the ability to pass through the walls. She held herself back from creating her own route through the rock, for she did not know how strong her stones were yet, and if she exhausted herself she would be in serious trouble. Instead, she headed through the silent corridors, drawing nearer and nearer the surface with every step.

Another thick metal door separated the corridor network from the shaft that led up to the top level. She tried out her keys until she found one that fitted, and then paused for a time, sensing ahead. There were no Crawlers above. Maybe they had something else? Yes, she could feel footsteps, but it was difficult to locate them with any degree of accuracy without devoting her entire attention to it, and she was still out of practice. She had to stay mobile.

Is this what you want? she asked, addressing the question to the invisible helper that was manipulating her. There was no reply. She opened the door, stepped into the shaft and locked it behind her.

It was a dark tube of rock that she stood in, not much wider than her shoulders. A set of metal rungs had been driven into the stone on one side, leading to a doorway forty feet above. A lone glowstone nestled at the top of the shaft, its light barely reaching down to where Kia stood. With the weapon still held in one hand – the *hooking-flail* (was that what it was called? It just seemed to fit) – she climbed up.

The corridor was empty beyond the door, but there was something different about this level. It took her a short time to realize what it was. Her breath was no longer steaming the air; it was warm here. She looked up at the thick black pipes of iron that ran along the ceiling, and noticed the beads of condensation that dripped from their grimy surfaces. Steam-pipes, to drive some kind of Machinist mechanism; that was the source of the heat.

Like they've got in Tusami City, came the thought, and then darted away before she could wonder at its source.

Footsteps were approaching.

She heard them with a jolt of alarm, and

looked over her shoulder at the door from the shaft. She'd closed it and locked it behind her, and now she had no time to find the key again. The pipes! She peered upward, and saw that there was a gap between the rock ceiling and the black–iron skin of the pipes. Hurriedly, she reached up and jumped to lay her hand against one of them. Hot, but not unbearable.

She clambered up.

The Taskmaster turned the corner, his scimitar held loosely in one hand, betraying his caution. Hadn't he heard something, the sound of a lock turning? In the silence of night, broken only by the occasional distant rumble of the Crawlers from below, his hearing had sharpened so that even the slightest noise was enough to alert him. Not that any of the workers had ever got up here before, but then that made it even more unusual that he should hear such a sound.

The tunnel appeared to be empty. The flat grey rectangle of the door that led to the shaft stood closed.

But he still couldn't shake that nagging

suspicion, the intuition that something was wrong.

Cautiously, he moved down the corridor.

Kia held her breath as the Taskmaster walked beneath her, visible through the gaps between the pipes. She was running with sweat, for she was still wearing layers of furs and the warmth of her hiding-place had quickly heated them up. What was he looking for? He could *see* there was nobody in the corridor. She had wedged herself between the rock ceiling and the pipes, a gap of a few feet left to allow airflow; but what had been a snap decision had turned out to be a potentially bad one. She was stuck here, with no way to manoeuvre or escape.

Should have just gone through the rock, she told herself, but she knew that would have been an even worse idea. There was nothing on either side of this tunnel, and she couldn't just walk through solid rock without an immense amount of concentration and effort. The Taskmaster would surely have caught her.

She just had to hang on a little longer, and hope the guard would go away.

The Taskmaster tried the handle of the door. Locked, as it should be. So why was he worried? It was that sensation, that feeling that something was amiss. Like he was being watched.

Unable to help himself, he turned his head and looked over his shoulder, up the tunnel, in case anyone was creeping up on him. Nothing. He laughed softly at his own jumpiness, dismissing his fears, and was about to return to his patrol when he flinched as something tiny and wet struck him in the face, just below his nose.

Condensation from the pipes, he thought. The cursed things were always dripping on him. Absently, he licked his upper lip, and then hesitated.

Not the usual metallic, dirty tang of the pipes. This was salty. This was *sweat*.

Kia felt a thrill of cold terror race through her as the Taskmaster looked up, his dreadlocks falling back from his masked face, his dark eyes angry and alert, already aware of her presence. Their gazes met through the tiny sliver of orange light between the pipes, and then she cried out and pulled herself aside as he thrust his scimitar through the gap. The second strike was inaccurate, glancing off metal. Kia scrambled to free herself where she was wedged, beads of perspiration flying from her hair, but the thick furs around her foiled her. Beneath her, the Taskmaster was lining up for a third stab.

Concentrate, she thought, and the stone of the tunnel leaped to respond.

The Taskmaster shouted in surprise as a thin column of rock burst from the wall, darting out and swallowing his hand, engulfing his knuckles and the hilt of his scimitar in a cold grip. His shout turned into a scream as he felt the bones in his hand crack under the immense pressure, and then the column suddenly retreated back into the wall, pulling him hard with it. He smashed into the stone and slumped to the ground, unconscious, his broken hand released.

Kia clambered hastily down from her ill-advised hiding place, almost treading on the supine form of the guard as she slipped down to the tunnel floor. Stupid, *stupid!* That scream would bring anybody near by running. She should have taken him out straight away.

No choice now. She would just have to run. And so she did, up the corridor in the direction the guard had come from. The skin of her face was flushed, dark in the dull orange light, and her back and legs prickled infuriatingly under her furs. She wished she could throw off some of the many layers that she wore, but she would need them if she got to the surface, for the desert would be bitingly cold. She would have to endure; and if she had learned anything during the year she had spent in the mines, it was endurance.

The tunnel split into two up ahead, and running footsteps were approaching from one of them. She halted for a moment, trying to determine where the sound was coming from, but the hollow echo made it impossible. She took the left passage, following the original route she had planned, and almost immediately the footsteps seemed to disappear as they were dampened by the rough walls.

Lucky, she thought, and sprinted onward, the hooking-flail swinging from her gloved fist, her shadow long in the dim orange. *Now, there should be a turn-off about . . . here.*

Her prediction was good. The passage was broken by a second, smaller tunnel off to her left. Her heart thudded in her chest as she took it. The sounds of a general alarm were rising all about her now. She was beginning to panic; this was only the second time she had disobeyed the Taskmasters, and the first time that she could remember her life being in danger.

"Hoi!" came a cry from behind her, and she swore as she saw two Taskmasters emerge from a doorway. They immediately gave chase, the wicked blades of their scimitars sliding free of their belts, hollering for their companions.

"Shut *up!*" Kia screamed, throwing out a hand behind her. A shockwave blasted up the corridor, a great pulse that tore along the walls and floor and ceiling, blowing a cloud of loose dirt and stone in its wake. It hit the Taskmasters and threw them off their feet, their scimitars scraping away across the stone. They scrabbled to their feet, one of them running away with a frightened yelp.

But the other had clenched his fists, holding

them before him, and Kia felt the sudden surge of Flow as his stones powered up. She sensed what was coming a moment before it hit her: she had experienced it several times before, though not for a long time now. The Taskmasters' spirit-stones were purple and grey: torturer's stones. They possessed the power to inflict pain.

The initial twisting in her gut was like a punch in the stomach, but what followed was worse. A terrible wrench, as if someone was tearing her intestines roughly out of her belly; and then climbing her oesophagus, squeezing her trachea from the inside, closing up her throat, preventing her from breathing. She dropped to her knees, hands clawing at her neck, tears of pain blurring her vision as she gagged.

The Taskmaster shrieked, and then suddenly the agony was gone.

She coughed convulsively for a few moments, her face a few inches from the floor as she hovered between retching and gasping for air. She looked up, getting shakily to her feet, and a flinch of surprise crossed her face as she saw what had become of the Taskmaster. In fact, she was no longer sure it *was* the Taskmaster. The bloodied mass of gore that was spread across the tunnel could have been anything.

Did I do that? she asked herself, distantly. *Or was it my helper?* She really didn't care. All she wanted to do was get out of here now.

But she would *never* let one of her jailors use their stones on her again. The cold flame inside her flared into a blaze as the fear dissipated and was replaced by anger. She'd held back twice now, and both times she'd nearly paid with her life. Next time, she would kill first and think of mercy later.

She got to her feet and ran again, her steps lent strength by the tightly controlled rage that consumed her. A door was opening in the corridor just ahead; she whirled the hooking-flail once and buried it in the head of the man who came through before he was even aware that she was there. She left the weapon entangled in his dreadlocks; it was too clumsy for her, unfamiliar. Anyway, if she had her directions right, she was almost at the—

There it was. The cargo elevator, a great,

steam-driven platform that sat at the bottom of an enormous, diagonally-sloping shaft on the far end of an immense cavern. Stacks of boxes, crates, and tarpaulin-covered heaps of tools and machinery stood around the floor. From behind her, she could hear the sound of the Taskmasters approaching along the tunnel, no doubt summoned by the one who had run from her shockwave.

She hurried into the cavern and turned back to the tunnel that she had entered from. Splaying her fingers, she reached out her hand to it . . . and snapped it shut. The rock convulsed and belched inward, collapsing into the mouth of the tunnel in a rising wreath of dust, blocking it completely.

Across the empty cavern she went, her furs making her unbearably hot, her tangled hair sodden with sweat. She had made it three-quarters of the way across when the pain hit her again, like burning claws being dragged down her back. She shrieked, stumbling onward, not knowing where the fire was coming from. . .

"You think we're going to let one of you get away?" came the voice, deep and throaty. "You know what King Macaan will *do* to us if we allow you to escape, Mi'atte?"

"*Kia!*" she shouted, and then fell to the ground as her legs spasmed and locked. "My name's Kia, you. . ."

"Kia? Really? The King has been looking for you for a long time," said the voice, piqued with interest. "Well, I am the Overseer of this facility, Kia. And it is my job to ensure that nobody escapes their just punishment."

He stepped out from behind a stack of crates, a tall man with a build like Hochi's. (Hochi? Who was he?) His skin was heavily tanned from the desert sun, and he wore a black fur vest over his expansive belly. His heavily muscled arms were crossed over his chest, and his head was completely bald, with a rubbery toad-face that smirked at her as he emerged.

She recognized him now. The man that the slavers had sold her to.

"You know I'm not here for any punishment!" she spat. "You *bought* me!"

"And what an investment," came the reply, accompanied by a fresh twist of agony in her chest, as if her heart had wrapped around itself and tugged tight. "If you really *are* Kia, you'll be a fine present for the King."

She gasped in a breath. He was keeping her writhing, not allowing her to gather her concentration, to focus her power. But each new pain brought her a greater anger, and her teeth clenched as she fought to resist him. She was on her hands and knees, straining as if something enormous was sitting on her back.

"Don't waste your time, little girl. You can't possibly bring your powers to bear."

"No," she said, fighting to raise her head and look him in the eyes. "I just can't *focus*."

A frown crossed his brow, and a flicker of worry came into his expression.

She released all of her remaining power at once, letting it all go with no shape and no form. From her huddled, crouched form a shockwave blasted out in all directions, crashing through the cavern in a great ripple. The rock cracked and groaned as it was shifted, shedding great boulders from the walls and ceiling. The Overseer ducked instinctively, but the ground swell threw him off his feet and he could only wail a final cry of fear as the stack of crates that he had been concealed behind came toppling down on him.

Curled up, her hands over her head, Kia thought of nothing, her mind a blank. Chance, hope, those things were the only factors for her survival. The boulders that were being shaken loose from the ceiling of the cavern were crashing down all around her, even the smallest ones arriving at a lethal velocity. She flinched and whimpered as one hit close enough to pepper her with stone shards, and squeezed her eyes tight, praying to whatever forces governed her fate that she would not be killed now, it would be unfair, *so* unfair. . .

And then it stopped. The thumping diminished to a loose rattle of pebbles, and silence returned to reign again in the cavern. For a time, she did not dare to look up; but when she did, she saw the damage she had wreaked all around her. The neatly stacked crates were in disarray; tools were scattered about; and everywhere, rocks and rubble.

But she was *alive*.

An uncontrollable smile breaking out on her face, she got to her feet; but her smile faded as her body dragged her back down to the ground, an unnatural ache of exhaustion settling into her bones. Stone-drained, she had tired herself to the limits of her muscles.

Someone I knew always used to do that . . . someone. . .

No time now. She fought against the crippling lethargy and dragged herself along the floor, making for the cargo elevator.

Please . . . just one more piece of good luck . . . don't let me have broken the elevator. . .

Slowly, the tendons of her neck taut with exertion, she crawled the short distance to the lip of the elevator's main platform. It had been buckled, and some of the metalwork above looked loose, but it had apparently stayed firm as the rock beneath it warped. Maybe.

A small control panel with a brass lever stood at the near edge of the platform. With a last marshalling of the feeble amount of strength she had left, she slung an arm to it and shoved it into the up position.

Come on, come on. . .

A great blast of steam boiled up with a hiss as the pressure-jets kicked in, and the elevator lurched upwards, stopped . . . and then began a steady ascent, sliding diagonally up the shaft, guided by spiked cogs on its side that slotted into metal indentations in the wall. Kia hitched a sigh, slumping to the floor of the platform, swathed in the heat of her furs as the temperature began to drop. Glowstones slid by her closed eyes, periodically lighting up her lids in orange and then fading as she rested, drifting towards sleep.

. . .can't sleep yet can't sleep yet just a little further. . .

The elevator rocked to a stop with another hiss, and the dissipating steam rose around her in a cloud. She opened her eyes in time to see the enormous metal gate rising slowly in front of her with a whine of hydraulics, allowing in the cold night air, lifting higher and higher to reveal the empty blue dunes of the desert humping away into the distance.

That, and the two figures that walked in from

outside to crouch down next to her. A man and a woman, dressed in furs not unlike her own.

"Kia?" said the woman, her face in shadow. She smelled of sweet desert-flowers.

Kia croaked an affirmative.

"We meet at last," the woman continued, a smile lifting her voice.

The man reached down and slid his arms under her, and lifted her like a child. She hooked her own arms around his neck, too weak to do anything but go along with him.

"Let's move," said the woman, standing. "We have a long way to go."

Kia closed her eyes and buried her face in the furs of the man's chest, and began to weep.

3

The Prospect of their Freedom

"So here we are," said Gerdi, scanning the great, empty plain before him, pale blue under the eclipsed light of the Kirin Taq sun. "Looks like you got had."

Calica joined him on the crest of the low rise of land, the last remnants of the hills that they had been travelling over before they flattened out into an immense swathe of empty grassland that stretched to the horizon. Small, crystalline bunches of flowers chimed softly in the breeze, and the Glimmer plants that grew in every corner of Kirin Taq dotted the darkness in sparse clusters, glowing violet at their core.

"They'll be here," she said, fingering the turquoise gem that rested against her breastbone.

To the left and right of them, the shuffling click of the Keriags heralded the presence of their escort; fifty of the insectile creatures, all told. And with them, Jaan and Iriqi, the enormous Koth Taraan. They stood in a line across the crest, looking out across the ethereal vastness of the plain, and waited.

Calica's face was impassive as she looked into the distance, her thoughts far away. Kirins had no way of measuring years – years were meaningless without day or night, winter or summer. So instead they divided their time into cycles, governed by the rotation of the colours of the Glimmer plants, which pulsed in sync all across the land. These they bunched into hundred-cycles and thousand-cycles.

Each cycle was approximately equivalent to a Dominion day. It had been around seven hundred-cycles since the Integration, when the Parakkan army had been thrown into Kirin Taq. Roughly three hundred-cycles since the Princess Aurin had been defeated, and Calica had become the bearer of the heartstone that held the future of the Keriag race between its clear, blueish-green

41

facets. Just over two hundred-cycles since Ryushi had Bonded with a wild wyvern.

Two Dominion years she had spent in this darkened land. And as beautiful as it was, as serene and elegant as it might be, she wanted nothing more at this moment than to be standing in the stifling, muggy heat of a market in Tusami City, breathing the dust and feeling the hot, wonderful rays of the Dominion sun on her skin.

The stone that hung around her throat dragged at her with the weight of her responsibility. She cursed the day when it had been revealed that she was the Splitling of the tyrant Princess, when she had become the only person who could prevent Aurin's lethal gem from cracking and precipitating the mass extinction of the Keriags. How could she have known the chain of events that revelation would set into motion? As if she had been given a choice. . .

In the days following Aurin's defeat (and she used the word *days* purposefully, for the moment she started to think in Kirin time was the moment when she gave up hope of ever returning to the light) the Council of Parakka had been in uproar.

There were those who called for the immediate invasion of the Dominions, to oust Macaan while he was still reeling from the loss of his power over the Keriags, which had formed the bulk of his army. With the Koth Taraan and many Kirins willing to help, Macaan would be unable to prevent Parakka gaining a strong foothold. An almost equally weighted faction advocated a careful gathering of troops, so as not to charge in recklessly; there was not enough information yet about the King's forces, and it was pointed out that the Keriag Queens had refused to help them against Macaan in the Dominions, for the Keriags preferred their native land of Kirin Taq and wanted as little to do with human affairs as they possibly could. Calica could not blame them, after what Macaan had done.

In the end, the Keriags made the decision for them.

Before her death at the hands of Takami, Kia had tried to persuade Calica to use the heartstone as Aurin had – to enslave them, and use them to drive Macaan from the face of the Dominions. Calica had refused. But the Keriags, it seemed, were not willing to trust the survival of their species to one person's word, no matter who it was.

Within a few cycles of Aurin's downfall – known to history as the Battle of Fane Aracq – the Keriag Queens had sent Parakka an ultimatum, using the Koth Taraan as their translators. Until a way could be found to deactivate the heartstone, no war was to be made on Macaan. The Ley Warrens – the only bridges between the two worlds – would be as closely guarded against the Parakkans as they were against Macaan's troops. Part of it was to ensure that the Parakkans did not forget their half of the deal made between Kia and the Keriag Queens, that the heartstone should be deactivated and the Keriags freed. After all, the safety of the Keriags was of little importance to most of the humans, especially as they were known as hated and vicious enemies to the Kirins.

It was because the Keriags' lives meant so little to the greater portion of Parakka that another factor had been all but overlooked in the rush of preparation for war. If Macaan died, the trigger-stone in his forehead would crack the heartstone that Calica wore, and the Keriags would die with him. The Keriag Queens could not take the risk that Parakka would win against Macaan, for their lives were as inextricably linked with his as with Calica's. No assurance would be enough for them that Macaan's life would be spared. It was not uncommon for rulers to take their own lives rather than surrender to capture; King Oko of the Dominions had done it when Macaan had destroyed his Knights and deposed him.

So, stalemate. Calica was forced either to become like Aurin, resorting to slavery to make the Keriags co-operate, or to accede to their demands.

I never asked for any of this, she thought, and then a flicker of disgust crossed over her face. Self-pity was not an acceptable option.

"Calica? Hey bug-lady, you alright?" Gerdi asked, nudging her in the thigh with his elbow. Gerdi's characteristic lack of tact meant he used the nickname as a joke, blithely unaware of how much it hurt Calica.

"Make camp," she said absently, still looking out over the plain. "We wait until they decide to join us."

Gerdi scratched the back of his neck and ruffled his shock of bright green hair. "Not exactly renowned for being punctual, are they? You think they're gonna show?"

"If they show, they show," she said, falsely casual. "You don't dictate terms to the Deliverers."

They pitched at the edge of the plains, a small cluster of hide tents surrounded by a circle of Keriags. The insectile creatures stood motionless, facing outwards, their low-slung torsos hanging between their six spiderlike, chitinous legs, their serrated *gaer bolga* spears held ready. A fire of smokeless wychwood burned between the tents, lighting the faces, chests and laps of those sat around it, the bright yellow glow a contrast to the cool blue-velvet of the dark. A soft wind gusted across the plain, gently teasing across their backs, making the flames lean one way or another.

"They spook me when they're like this," Gerdi said, glancing around at their frozen guardians.

((They were told by the hive-mind to keep guard. They will not move, eat, or do anything

else until their orders or their situation are changed. It is in their nature)) Iriqi's voice came from directly inside their heads. Over the last few hundred-cycles, the young Koth Taraan had learned to keep the emotional colours out of its thoughts, except when it wanted to convey something. With Jaan, however, it never held back. The two of them were too close for that.

"Are they talking now?" Calica asked, gazing distractedly into the fire.

Iriqi shifted its huge weight. It was sitting in the neutral position that members of its race always seemed to adopt when resting, slightly slouched forward in a half-crouch. *((They are always talking. The Queens are agitated at the prospect of their freedom))*

"I thought you'd be excited, Calica," Jaan said, brushing his matted ropes of hair back over his shoulder.

Calica looked over at the half-breed, who was regarding her curiously with his disconcerting saffron eyes from within his coffee-coloured face, and shrugged wearily. "I'm just tired," she said. "It's been a long year."

And so it had. Since the Battle of Fane Aracq, Calica had travelled the length and breadth of Kirin Taq with an assortment of different companions, always searching for one thing: a Deliverer. Aurin had told Ryushi that a Deliverer had the power to deactivate the heartstone and free the Keriags at last. All they had to do was find one.

How easy it had sounded then. But it was only as the cycles wore on that Calica had realized just how little anybody knew of the Deliverers. Where they came from, how they lived, what their purpose was . . . all these things were mysteries. All that was clear was that they possessed some kind of super-sense that told them when they were needed, when the time for an infant's *pah'nu'kah* – the ceremonial implantation of their spirit-stones – was at hand. Silent, aloof, they were regarded less as sentient beings and more as a part of the cycle of Dominion life, as much as the actual birth or the child's coming of age.

But where there were no spirit-stones, there were no Deliverers.

And that was the crux of the problem. Macaan

had long choked the supply of spirit-stones in Kirin Taq by closing all the mines and allowing only nobles and those Guardsmen assigned to their armies to possess them. Their services in so little demand, the Deliverers had disappeared from Kirin Taq some time ago. It had been revealed by the deposed thanes after the Battle of Fane Aracq that nobles had to travel to the Dominions if they wanted a *pah'nu'kah* for their child, and that most of their Guardsmen were Dominion-folk instead of native Kirins, because only Dominion-folk were implanted with stones as infants any more.

But Macaan had been in the process of implementing the same measures in the Dominions after the Integration. Not to the same extent – for he had kept three mines open to supply only his nobles or those that had sworn their children to his service – but enough so that the number of *pah'nu'kah* ceremonies had dropped drastically. And so had the number of Deliverers. Until, a year ago, shortly after Aurin had been deposed . . . they disappeared altogether.

49

Not that this stopped Macaan keeping the mines in operation. Apart from the fact that it was still the most dreaded punishment in the land, he was building quite a stockpile of dormant stones against the time when the Deliverers might return.

Why did they go? she thought to herself. There had still been a need for them; hundreds of *pah'nu'kah* ceremonies a year had to be carried out for Macaan's future troops. Admittedly, it was nothing to the thousands that were customary when the common folk were allowed access to stones, but still. . .

Who knew what went on inside the heads of the Deliverers? All she knew was that they had been absent for many months, and there were fears that they would never come back.

Until ten cycles ago, when they had all but given up hope.

A sudden skittering rippled across the black ranks of the Keriags, like a breeze through the leaves of a tree. All of them looked up from the fire, Gerdi springing to his feet.

((Something is happening)) said Iriqi, a fizzing

orange swipe of excitement with a bruise-violet blot of trepidation accompanying the statement.

Jaan and Calica jumped up and joined Gerdi in looking out across the plain. The Keriag formation had tightened around them, shuffling protectively closer; but as their bodies hung near to the ground, the humans could see easily through the high, thin stick-legs of the creatures. Iriqi, ten feet tall, stood where it was and watched with its huge, teardrop-shaped alien eyes.

The plain was still and empty.

"What? I don't see anything."

((They sense something)) Iriqi said, being the only one who could hear the Keriag's silent relays. *((I sense it too))* he added.

Something *was* happening on the plain, a faint shimmering nearby, as of white light playing on a shallow film of lapping, perfectly clear water. The disturbance was small, and only a few dozen yards away from them. And something was resolving there, a shape, beginning as a blurred smudge of several colours and slowly sharpening into focus, slowly, until. . .

"So *that's* how they do it," said Gerdi, awed.

51

Standing before them was a Deliverer. His hair was shaved into black stripes that hugged the contours of his bald skull. His leather mask hid his lower face from view, leaving only his fiercely intense eyes under thick brows. He wore a motley of robes and furs, so thick that they made him seem twice as broad in the shoulder as he actually was. There was no apparent indicator of rank, and one Deliverer looked almost indistinguishable from another. Silent. Anonymous. Unfathomable.

The Keriags parted, moving in harmony to clear a path for Calica. The others waited where they were as she walked forward, each step seeming to make her body lighter until she felt her heart could lift her up off the grass.

They actually came, she thought. *Can it really be over?*

"Greetings to you, honoured lord Deliverer," she said, her voice clear and strong. "I am Calica, leader of the Maar Chapter of Parakka. We are here at the appointed place to beg your most generous assistance in the dispensation of Princess Aurin's evil legacy."

The words hung in the air, swallowed by the silence of the plains. The Deliverer did not move a muscle, merely stared at her with his burning gaze.

Behind him, the plains began to shimmer.

Gerdi swallowed back an oath. The whole of the immense grassland before them was glimmering with rippling light, spreading many dozens of metres high. Never before had he seen an event of such a scale, except when the Ley Booster exploded during the Integration and flipped the entire Parakkan army into Kirin Taq. Open-mouthed, they gaped as something massive began to shimmer into focus, something so big that their eyes could not take it all in, tightening into clarity before them.

And then it was done. And they stood there before the city of the Deliverers.

4

In No Place, and at No Time

The wind plucked and tore at Ryushi as he whooped in exultation, hunched low over the back of his Bond-wyvern, Araceil. Araceil screeched in response, swooping down into the canyon to join the rest of the flight. They were gliding in an arrowhead formation, soaring along a deep gash in the Fin Jaarek mountain range under the hollow corona of the Kirin Taq sun. Unquiet clouds loomed overhead, and a whirling gale raced down the trenches between the mountains.

Araceil allowed Ryushi to ease him into position at the back and left of the A-shaped arrangement, matching speed with the other five wyverns in the flight. It was a curiously mutual thing; Araceil needed Ryushi to guide him as little as Ryushi needed to tell his wyvern where to go. The two of them knew each other's thoughts on an instinctive level, through the diamond-shaped Bonding-stones that sheened red on their foreheads.

Up ahead, the canyon suddenly fractured into a maze of rock pillars and juts, a complex mess of old riverways and shattered pieces of the mountains from some upheaval long past, dark and shady in the dim light. Ryushi felt a smile curl his lips as they swept towards it, battling to stay in position against the wind that blasted around them. Somewhere to his right, one of the others tipped a wing too far and was swept out of formation by a few metres, before adjusting to correct his position and return to a steady path.

Ryushi had come to love these training manoeuvres. Ever since his wyvern had reached adulthood – and a wyvern's growth period was incredibly short and fast, for they reached full size within a hundred and fifty cycles of hatching – he had been flying with the Parakkan forces on their practice sorties. And if Araceil was a little young and immature when they first began, the shortfall was compensated for by the fact that Ryushi had been flying wyverns for a good few years back in the Dominions, having grown up on a wyvern stud, and that put him ahead of most other riders his age. The two of them were a good team.

At the front of the formation, the lead rider raised one fist as they winged closer to the rocky maze.

"You ready?" Ryushi said, his fingers poised on the nerve-points at the base of Araceil's long neck. They affected the wyvern's forewings, which in turn manipulated the airflow past the larger hind wings to steer. The scales had been rubbed off there for greater sensitivity.

The fist dropped, and the formation broke, wheeling into a cluster and then dissolving into six dark bolts of speed as they headed for their chosen entrance to the trial zone. The smooth and controlled formation flying was done; now it was a race to the end, to be the first one to negotiate the tricky canyon and emerge from the other side.

"Go! Go! Go!" Ryushi shouted at Araceil, who screeched excitedly as he tore into the space between two thick fingers of stone and then banked hard right, slicing across one of the other riders' flight path and causing him to dive sharply to avoid a collision, yelling a curse. They corkscrewed through a gaping hole in a great fin of rock – a short, rough tunnel – and the sudden pressure change caused the blood to whine in Ryushi's ears. Then they burst free, his ears popping, and carved left to find themselves racing along a deep, knife-slash trench a few dozen metres behind their flight leader, Jikkio.

"*That's* our girl!" Ryushi shouted over the rush of wind. Jikkio was the fastest and most able flyer of the six of them; if they could get ahead of her, they didn't need to worry about the others.

Araceil screeched again, issuing a challenge to the lead wyvern. Jikkio looked back over her shoulder, her black hair streaming and flapping across her face, and smiled.

Rushing towards them was another rocky jut, branching out left and right to join with its neighbours. Jikkio banked down and left; Ryushi up and right, spurring Araceil to even greater speeds. The rocks closed in, and Araceil was buffeted by the howling, swirling gale that roared headlong into them. He narrowed his wings, streamlining, and they swooped down low to avoid the violent current of air that was being concentrated in their tight valley.

Clever girl, Ryushi thought. *She knew this route would be like a wind tunnel in this kind of weather.*

Then, to his left, he saw a small break in the rock wall. Araceil noticed it a moment later, instinctively picking up on his rider's thoughts. A question, communicated not in words but in something less tangible: *shall we go for it?* Stay and fight through the wind, playing safe but losing time, or take the risk? The decision was agreed in a fraction of a second. The wild-born wyvern and his rider were just as brash and reckless as each other.

The timing would be crucial at this kind of speed, and in these conditions.

Just . . . about . . . NOW!

The sudden sweep left shifted the wind shear on to Araceil's underside, propelling them sideways and blowing them through the gap in the rock and into the calmer air on the other side. Araceil, his wings spread to full extent, glided smoothly back level and then thrust forward, accelerating hard to make up lost time.

The canyons and juts, protrusions and obstacles, blurred past them as they dived and weaved, swiping through narrow gaps and winging down chicanes. They were both pushing it dangerously hard, eager to win, cutting close to the unforgiving rock and nearly clipping it several times. The shadowy walls loomed night-blue under the faint light of the Kirin Taq sun. Their hearts pounded in unison as they dodged and banked, never letting themselves relax for a second, until. . .

"*Got*cha!" Ryushi cried as they blasted out of a thick crevice and appeared head-to-head next to Jikkio in the long, straight canyon that marked the final run. She looked across at him, an expression of surprise on her face; and then she hardened with determination, and hugged lower to her wyvern, spurring it forward.

Araceil responded even before Ryushi had, picking up his pace almost to the limit of his ability. Ryushi followed Jikkio's lead, making himself as small and streamlined as possible so as not to hinder his mount. This was Araceil's show now; he was not going to let the rival wyvern beat him.

They tore low along the canyon, correcting themselves periodically as a capricious gust of wind tried to knock them around, both creatures flying flat out to win. But Jikkio's mount was in its prime; formidably fast, older and more experienced than Araceil. She was slowly pulling ahead.

"Come on, we can *beat* them," Ryushi muttered, knowing that Araceil felt the sentiment even if he did not hear the words.

The end of the canyon was coming up fast, and still they were losing ground.

The idea hit Ryushi and Araceil at the same time, and both responded in unison; Ryushi dug in on Araceil's nerve-points and the wyvern responded, slowing and swooping left, scraping frighteningly close to the rival wyvern before settling at a point directly behind it, a little way back. Here, in the slipstream of the other creature, the wind resistance was much less. Araceil began to accelerate again, beating his massive, leathery wings as hard as he could, picking up speed and closing on Jikkio's mount faster and faster, while the end of the canyon loomed nearer and nearer. . .

"Now!" Ryushi cried, and Araceil darted upward, out of the slipstream. The extra speed he had picked up behind his rival carried him forward, overtaking the other creature as both of them climbed hard, and he burst from the canyon neck and forewings ahead of Jikkio, spiralling into the sky with a triumphant shriek before levelling into an exhausted glide.

Jikkio moved into position alongside them. Ryushi looked over at her, a breathless grin on his face. Jikkio tilted her head at him, and saluted with a wry smile, before peeling off to watch the others arrive.

For a long while, Ryushi hung in the air with Araceil, enjoying the mutual feeling of victory. He ran a finger along the red, diamond-shaped Bonding-stone on his forehead, and gave a contented sigh, before heading down to where

Jikkio was reassembling the flight formation for the journey home.

~we must undo what has been done~

The Deliverer's voice was so low that Calica could barely hear it, a gargling, guttural croak. The meaning of the words were lost amid the implications of the sound itself; a Deliverer was *speaking*!

The Deliverer had invited the humans and the Koth Taraan into their city, but the Keriags had refused to enter for reasons of their own. Now the five of them walked with their host through the thoroughfares of a place never before seen by any non-Deliverer in recorded history, and Calica was beginning to dare to hope that her search had ended at last.

The city soared all around them as they walked through it. It was awesome, unlike anything they had seen before in Kirin Taq or the Dominions. The fusion of construction, nature and machinery was chaotic and cluttered the sky wherever they looked. Here, a massive bunch of metal cables wound their way up the bole of an immense, ancient tree with a green, leathery skin. There, a wooden platform and set of huts sat in the branches of another tree, while at ground level the trunk had been surrounded by some kind of shrine, made of carven stone and delicate glass. A shanty of tents sat next to the humping metal bulk of a factory. A hundred different styles of architecture clashed and collided in an untidy mess, meshing with the huge trees that rose all around them.

"This place is screwed up!" Gerdi commented happily, glutted with new sights.

((There are examples of buildings and machines from all ages of Kirin history)) said Iriqi. ***((And even Koth Taraan))***

Jaan looked up, and there, indeed, was a pile of the large ceramic mud-igloos that the Koth Taraan dwelt in. "The Communion told you that, huh?" he asked, referring to the network of collective race memory that Iriqi shared with every member of his species.

~the city was built over many thousands of years~ said the Deliverer who walked with them. *~we preserve everything we make~*

"Doesn't the wood rot? Or the stone decay?" Calica asked, more to make conversation to ease her own nerves than from any real desire to know.

~time does not pass here as it does outside~ came the whispered, gurgling reply. ~i myself was present when that building was built~

They looked at the one he indicated; it was little more than a slanted long hut of hard-baked mud and straw over a framework of branches, and a roof of wattle and daub.

A splash of bright red amazement from Iriqi coloured their minds.

~as your Koth Taraan companion has guessed, that was built many hundreds of Dominion years ago~

"That would mean you . . ." Gerdi began, then cut himself off before he stated the obvious and muttered: "And I thought Hochi was getting on. . ."

"Why have your people never talked before?" Calica asked their host.

~we do not speak outside our home, unless in the direst of times~ he said.

"Why not?" Jaan interjected.

~we hold too many secrets~ came the reply.

"So why have you brought us here now?"

~a balance must be restored~ he said, and that was the end of it.

The Parakkan effort to bring back the Deliverers had begun as soon as their Resonant spies had revealed that they had disappeared from the Dominions. The first step had been to reopen the mines in Kirin Taq; but this time, it was not as a punishment. Miners were to be paid as in any job, as they had been in the Dominions before Macaan arrived. The job had the additional perk of a free spirit-stone for each five years of service. The prospect of being in the front line of the drive to improve their children's future – and help them prevent another Macaan from ever taking over – had Kirins flocking to the mines.

There were many disappointments. Many *pah'nu'kah* ceremonies were set up, but the Deliverers never came, and the newborn infant missed its chance for implantation. Calica and the Keriags had travelled far to try and track down the Deliverers; but to no avail. They hoped the

65

new influx of spirit-stones, the new need for the Deliverers, would tempt them out of hiding again; but really, what did they know of the Deliverer's motives? Why had they left in the first place, when there was still work for them to do? And would they return at all?

But then, news began to filter back to Parakka of isolated sightings, remote villages that *had* been visited. First they were few, but they were becoming steadily more common. The visitors vanished without trace and moved without leaving a trail. But once it had been established that the Deliverers were indeed back, it was decided that the time had come to set the lure.

Soon after, it was requested that any *pah'nu'kah* held in the central provinces was moved to Fane Aracq, the Princess's palace, which had become Parakka's base of operations. Several were held every day in the great hall; many people were willing to travel to the luxury of such grand surroundings.

For three cycles, the Deliverers had not shown. And then, on the fourth, one did. He arrived from nowhere, silently, stepping through the doors of the great hall even though the doormen had not seen him approach. He conducted the ceremony, ignoring all attempts to communicate with him, and ended by handing a scroll to the father of the newly-implanted baby. When he left, none dared to stop him.

The scroll was a map. The map led them to the plain. And so they had entered the city.

The Deliverer stood on the boarded wooden floor of the room and gazed at them with his fierce, dark eyes over a wide, shallow bowl of red liquid that rested on a metal plinth. The plinth was shot through with pipes and tiny, ratcheting levers and press-studs, and hummed steadily. The liquid shone like fire and gave out a warmth to match, sending burning ripples around the walls and thatched ceiling of the large, circular hut. There was no other light to see by; the Deliverer and those who stood by were bathed in a ruddy, arterial wash that rendered them as unearthly, bloodied ghosts.

This was only one of the many ceremonial huts that they passed on their way through the city. Calica could see no reason why this one had been chosen rather than any of the others; it was neither the biggest, nor the smallest, the most grand nor the most primitive. She had been preoccupied, anyway, watching the Deliverers go about their work all around them as they had travelled. Hundreds, thousands of them, all dressed in the furs and facemask that were the garb of their kind, all with the same strip-shaven hair, both Kirin and Dominion-born. Men and women were all but indistinguishable under their many layers of clothing. The most she had seen had been in one shrine or another, standing or sitting cross-legged in silent contemplation; they had seen dozens of different shrines, no two alike. But many others were occupied with menial tasks, carrying and chopping wood, constructing pipelines, digging ditches or cooking food. From what she could make out, they divided their time between working for their isolated, self-sufficient community and meditating. But the sights that they saw provided no clue as to the Deliverers' true purpose: why did they choose to live this way? And how had they hidden a whole city?

Now the four of them had been brought to stand before the bowl of liquid fire: two Dominion-folk, a halfbreed and a Koth Taraan. Six other Deliverers stood in the shadows around the room, motionless, watching. Their host, who had given them no name by which to call him, stood on the other side of the bowl, his masked face underlit by the red glow.

~you have questions~ came the dry rasp of a voice again. *~satisfy yourselves, then, before we proceed. you are the first who is not of our kind to be allowed into the city~*

Calica took a breath, torn between the desire to get on with the ceremony and rid herself of the terrible burden of the heartstone and her reluctance to waste a chance like this. Her hesitation allowed Gerdi to jump in first and make the choice for her.

"Why *did* you let us in?" he asked, cocking his head to one side, completely unfazed by the importance of the situation. "You never really said."

The Deliverer turned his dark eyes on to the young Noman boy. *~this ceremony is called the* ai'kie'shen. *it cannot be performed outside of this city. it cannot be performed in either Kirin Taq or the Dominions. the energy created would disrupt the fabric of existence~*

"Where *are* you gonna perform it, then?" Gerdi said.

~Netherfane~ was his answer. *~the Temple of the Void. the world of the Deliverers~*

"Uh-oh," Gerdi muttered. "Don't like the sound of that. When do we go?"

~ you are already there~

"What, really?" he said. He started for the door of the hut, which had been closed behind them, but one of the other Deliverers was standing with his arms crossed in front of it, barring him.

~you may not leave~ rasped their host. *~an untrained mind would unhinge in Netherfane. concepts such as time, spatial dimensions and what you call reality do not exist here. this hut is protected. outside lies madness~*

Gerdi looked uncertainly back at him, then at the door again. Finally, he shrugged and returned to Calica's side. "'Kay," he said.

~all Deliverers have the ability to traverse the

worlds, like Resonants do. think of Netherfane as the space between those worlds. we have the power to hold ourselves in that space, either partially or completely. to your eyes, we can become invisible, intangible, unsolid. it is how we deliver the spirit-stones, how we earn our name. this city is our home. it exists in no place, and at no time; it is everywhere and nowhere at once. no laws apply here. you are incapable of understanding~

"But why are you doing this for us?" asked Jaan, dwarfed by his Koth Taraan companion, who was observing and transmitting everything for the benefit of the Communion.

~the Deliverers are forbidden to intervene in the matters of the world. but a great wrong has been committed. we are bound to rectify it~

"What great wrong?" asked Calica.

~i cannot answer. you will know, in time~

There was a silence for a moment.

"What are the Deliverers?" Calica asked.

~we are the regulators. we are the equalizers. we keep the balance between the two worlds, that were separated in the great Sundering

*millennia ago. we see all futures, all possibilities.
we see what was, what is and what will be. we
are servants of the Flow, the life of the planets, the
network that stretches across stars you have yet to
see. our motives are deeper than we could
explain in your lifetime~*

"Why did you disappear?"

*~Macaan seeks to keep the spirit-stones for
himself and his own. it upsets the balance. we
will not aid him. spirit-stones are the planet's gifts
to its people. we, her servants, are given the
power to alter the nature of the stone according to
its recipient. it is the* pah'nu'kah~ He looked into
the bowl of red water. *~we see all futures~* he
repeated. Then he straightened once more. *~the
time has come to redress the balance. give me
the heartstone~*

Calica glanced at the others, seeking support
from their faces. Gerdi smiled encouragingly; Jaan
nodded; Iriqi was incapable of expressing
emotion physically, but it offered her a stout
mental bloom of royal blue, indicating solidarity.
She hooked her thumbs under her necklace to lift
it off, and paused. A thousand million lives rested

on this. Removing the turquoise stone from the thump of her heartbeat would mean it would crack in less than a cycle if it was not returned to her. She had not taken it off since she had put it on, a year ago, except to have a new clasp fitted. Ryushi had broken the first one tearing the necklace off Aurin.

Ryushi.

"Please be careful," she said. The Deliverer nodded gravely. She took it off and handed it to him.

Across two worlds, every Keriag stopped what it was doing and froze. The entire hive-mind of all the Queens was focused on one thing. The heartstone had been removed. They could sense the reaction in their own bodies, in the offspring stones that were buried in their flesh, waiting to kill them.

The Deliverer took the necklace and gently lowered the stone into the rippling liquid in the metal bowl.

~this device is an abomination~ he rasped, his eyes closing.

Abruptly, they felt the hum of the Flow swell

up around them, thickening the air. The clacking of the tiny switches and devices set in the pedestal became frenzied, and the Deliverer's gloved hands clenched tight on the necklace.

The water of the bowl was gradually turning blue, changing the light in the room from menacing to serene. Calica noticed that she had stopped breathing.

The Deliverer lifted the stone from the water and gathered it in both hands, holding it close to his chest like a treasured thing.

~it must be allowed to exist no longer~

With that, there was a loud crack, followed by a blast of energy like an explosion, a white wave of noise and force and—

Calica blinked. Not even their clothes or hair had been disturbed.

The Deliverer was holding out his hands, together at the wrist, palms upward. Against the black of his heavy gloves were a dozen sparkling turquoise shards.

~it is done~ he said. *~the link is broken. the Keriags are free~*

Calica felt a wave of dizziness sweep up to

claim her, but she forced it away. She would not faint, not even in the face of the overbearing, unbelievable relief and ecstasy that swamped her, or the immense exhaustion that settled on her shoulders. No longer was she the bearer. No longer the only thing between the Keriags and extinction.

She was unchained.

"Let's go see the Keriag Queens," she said to Iriqi. "I believe we have an invasion to begin."

5

For He was Breed

The wind-sirens howled through the corridors of the Machinists' Citadel. Everywhere, amid the perpetual clank and whine and chatter that never ceased inside its dark iron walls, footsteps and shouting could be heard. A crackly voice, its nuances lost somewhere between the mouth that it came from and the round speaker-grilles that broadcast it, was announcing instructions and calling the general alarm. Machinists hurried this way and that, a mix of fear, anger and confusion on those parts of their faces that had not been Augmented with metal or mechanisms.

Striding through it all, his mouth moving minutely beneath the chittering goggles of his eyes, his narrow chin hidden behind the high collar of his black greatcoat, was Corm. Only the flexing of his claw-hand and the restless whirr of the collection of minute tendons and tools around his wrist betrayed his agitation. He had a metal band that ran around the circumference of his bald head at eye level, replacing one ear with a circular bump that contained receiving equipment; his left cheek was covered in the same metal, and contained vibration sensors that could pick up and transmit sounds from the inside of his mouth. The transmitter/receiver were new additions to his arsenal of Augmentations, only installed after he had returned to the Citadel following the fall of Fane Aracq. As he walked, he was talking and listening, his voice little more than a mutter.

An explosion rocked the Citadel, making him stumble. He cursed and continued on, heading through the gloomy interior of the massive, enclosed construction that was the Machinists' home. As he issued orders, discussed suggestions and listened to reports, his thoughts were frantic, trying to sort and make sense of what was happening, seeking reasons and answers.

King Macaan was attacking the Machinists'

Citadel. The most well-defended fortress in the Dominions, and probably Kirin Taq as well. What plan did the tyrant have up his sleeve *now*?

There had been stories, of course. Stories about the King, about how the loss of his beloved daughter had driven him over the edge, that his always precarious sanity had crumbled with that final blow. Oh, he believed that Aurin was dead alright. After all, Fane Aracq had been stormed and Kirin Taq reclaimed; and if she had escaped, surely the Jachyra would have informed him by now.

But the Jachyra *did* know she was alive. Outside of a few members of Parakka and himself, they were the only ones who knew how Ryushi had allowed her to escape Fane Aracq before the Keriags arrived. The rest of Kirin Taq was told that she was slain in combat, partly to sate the Kirins' thirst for revenge for the cruel reign of the Princess, and partly because the Parakkans knew that the information would make its way back to Macaan sooner or later. Oh yes, the Jachyra knew. They just weren't telling him.

Corm was not sure what to believe. The King was as outwardly calm and enigmatic as he had ever been, but the reports of the Jachyra said that his private dealings with his aides were another story altogether. His mania for domination had always spoken of something not quite stable in his personality, and the loss of his parents, his queen, and now his daughter – in whom he had invested a great and hopeless love – would be enough to scar even the most resilient of men.

Insanity, though? No. There were many reasons why he might attack the Machinists' Citadel. And most chillingly, with the force that was now approaching from the east and south, he appeared to have the numbers to overwhelm it. But why, when he knew Parakka were massing their own forces? He had already lost the Keriags. Why risk crippling himself further, in the face of a possible invasion?

It was not that his move made no sense. It was just that the only thing he could think Macaan hoped to gain was too dreadful to contemplate.

Outside, the land was awash with Macaan's forces.

The Machinists' Citadel towered out of the plunging valleys, empty fens and treacherous crags that covered the west of the Dominions. These were wild highlands, with a cooler and wetter climate than the rest of the continent because of the cloud-bearing wind that blew all year round from the northwest, off the nearby coast. Like the flat steppes in the east, the arid deserts to the south and the mountains to the north, the west was sparsely settled compared with the fertile, temperate central mass of the land.

The Citadel stood alone on a great crag overlooking a deep, rocky valley, a tapering mountain of black iron. It bristled with turrets and cupolas that swivelled on automatic tracking systems to fix on the wyverns that circled and dived around it, the Artillerists on their backs punching force-bolts into the Citadel's metal skin. A ground battle was being waged on the landward side, where lumbering war machines assaulted each other relentlessly. Most of Macaan's machines had been originally bought from the Machinists' Guild, but the deactivation mechanisms they had installed against just this kind of attack had evidently been discovered and removed. All around ran clusters of Macaan's Guardsmen, clad in black armour, clutching their force-halberds.

Macaan's forces were many, a ragged swathe across the hills and valleys, but the Citadel was in an almost impenetrable position. Even with his military might, it would be a costly battle to win.

And then the guns went dead.

Corm stopped short as the deep, erratic whumphing of the Citadel's huge force-cannons suddenly diminished to nothing. A salvo of enemy bolts hammered the base, making him stagger against one wall; but he scarcely noticed, listening instead for the guns, waiting for them to start up again. When it became clear that they were not going to, he tapped a series of minute studs on his Augmented cheek.

"Core station, this is Corm. Report," he muttered. The sensors in the soft flesh of his inner cheek meant that he did not need to speak at normal volume to be heard.

"Corm! It's swarming down here! There's Jachyra everywhere! They're taking out the powerboards! Send someone!" There was a faint clatter, a few muffled shouts, and then static.

Corm's fingers ran over the studs again, zeroing in on a different frequency. "Secondary core. What's your status?"

"They're after the defences and the outer door locks," came a breathless reply. "Leaving all the interior systems intact. Someone told them exactly what to go for. They're trying to breach the main gates! We'll hold them off here as long as we can."

Corm tapped a stud to disconnect. So, what he had long suspected was true; Macaan *did* have spies deep in the Machinists' Citadel. They had probably been there for years, reporting on the growing unrest amid the dissenting Machinists who believed that one day Macaan would tire of paying for technology that he could simply take by force. It seemed that their paranoia had not been misplaced.

He did not blame Tatterdemalion or the Jachyra. The King's secret police were secretly loyal to Aurin, and he and Tatterdemalion were allies of a sort, but the Jachyra could never directly disobey Macaan. Like most of Macaan's top aides, they were implanted with stones during their Conversion that meant Macaan could kill them with a thought via the dark purple trigger-stone in his forehead. The King would not have got to be the ruler of two worlds without being as canny as he was ruthless.

Corm tapped another stud sequence, but that communication line was down. He cursed softly; even in this place, the most advanced technological marvel in the known worlds, malfunctions were rife.

Unless, of course, it wasn't a malfunction.

The thought sent a chill through his body. Turning on his heel, he strode quickly away through the bustling corridor. If Macaan was after the Pulse Hammer, then the Parakkan army would have more to fear than just his Guardsmen when they arrived in the Dominions. Much, much more.

Chiro should not have been away from his post. Should not, should not. But it had been a clash of priorities; what could he have done? He had been assigned to maintain and protect the Pulse Hammer. Maintain and protect. Neither one had been given more weight than the other in his orders; they were of equal importance.

So when he had gone to do routine maintenance work on the patch bay in the ducts that ran between the rooms of this section at floor level – he was the only one present who was small enough to fit – he had not been protecting the Pulse Hammer when the Guardsmen attacked. He had failed a part of his orders. But because he *had* failed, he was now the only one of his team left alive.

He watched as a pair of heavy, armoured black boots tramped past his hiding place, only a few inches from the mask that was his face. His eyes had automatically flicked to low-light vision to compensate for the pitch-black tunnel ducts, and he observed the room steadily in a grainy black and white.

The Pulse Hammer chamber was vast, an enormous shaft that ran up to a high, domed ceiling. Floor level was a chaotic jumble of stairs, lifts, banks of levers and switches, monitoring stations and generators. Above that, running along the edges of the shaft, were gantries and walkways. Most of the scaffolding that had surrounded the Pulse Hammer had been dismantled by now; after all, the preliminary tests were all complete, and all that remained was to start it up. The air was redolent of oil and steam – though not to Chiro, who had no olfactory sensors – and returned every sound with a metallic echo.

And then there was the Pulse Hammer itself. A thin obelisk of dark alloy metal, many dozens of metres high, its surface covered in panels, vents and innumerable small devices to facilitate its operation. At each of its corners, another obelisk stood, thinner and shorter, forming a square around the central pillar. At its base, four immense metal spheres were clustered, the generator chambers that would power the machine. It was a masterpiece of engineering, greater even than the Ley Boosters, reaching up through the massive shaft. The most accomplished Machinist device yet produced and the most complex. If it worked, of course.

All around the floor, sprawled at odd angles amid the blast-marks from their attackers' force-halberds, were the broken bodies of the operating staff. They had not conceded to the Guardsmen's demands for surrender, choosing instead a hopeless fight. Chiro approved. They had followed their orders. It was as it should be.

The receiver in his inner ear crackled suddenly. He did not flinch; he knew it was audible only to himself.

"Chiro! This is Corm. Why is the Pulse Hammer room line down?"

"The invaders have captured the Pulse Hammer," Chiro replied quietly. "Operational staff are dead. I am concealed and observing. Request further orders."

"What? How did they get *in*?"

"It seems probable that the Jachyra brought a small force with them through whatever portal they used," Chiro replied flatly. Most of the Machinists were educated enough about Macaan's secret police to know what they could do, unlike the larger proportion of the population. They knew the Jachyra could travel through mirrors; but it would have been ridiculously impractical to ban anything reflective from the interior of the Citadel.

There was a pause. "You are to render the Pulse Hammer non-functional, Chiro. Preferably without damaging it, but do it any way you can. Macaan must *not* be able to use it, Chiro. Make sure he can't return it to operational status, either."

"Suggest removing cortex key," Chiro said.

"Can you do it?"

"Pulse Hammer is not well guarded. Two sentries. Others have left to secure surrounding chambers."

"Then use any means necessary, and contact me for further instructions."

"Understood," Chiro replied, and his receiver went dead.

Good. Now he had direction, purpose, a definite goal. He was always happier that way. Happier? No, wrong word. Irrelevant emotion. It would be better to say that he was always more efficient with a single purpose to concentrate on.

He returned to his observation. It seemed likely

that there really were only a few Guardsmen inside the base, because the two sentries that they had left were pitifully inadequate for patrolling such a huge room. The banks of machinery would provide cover for him to get to the Pulse Hammer. He tried to calculate the probability of success, but his weak human brain was not up to the task of holding all the factors in his head.

Time was short. The longer he waited, the higher the chance of more Guardsmen arriving.

He pulled himself free from the duct, wriggling past the thick cables and pipes that pressed in on him. Out in the open, he padded across the room in a low crouch, keeping the bulk of the Pulse Hammer's support machinery between him and the slowly patrolling Guardsmen.

At a glance, he could have been taken as a young boy of about sixteen from the back, lean but not tall, with closely-shaved mousy hair and wearing dirty brown, sleeveless overalls. Maybe a casual observer, on getting a better look at him, might assume that he worked in an environment full of dangerous fumes; that would explain, at least, the flat planes of the mask that covered his face. It had an odd, slightly brassy sheen, with small, rectangular lenses for the eyes, and several cables appeared to run from it, over his shoulders and into the small, rounded silver pack on his back.

But it was only on seeing him close up that the observer would realize the cables were not running from the mask, but from the sides of his neck and under his jaw. And that the mask was not something he wore, it was part of his body, like the pack that was implanted in the flesh of his back, and the lenses that had replaced his eyes. And they would see the ridged lines of metal that slid in and out of the skin of his forearms and shoulders, and maybe wonder what else of this boy was Augmented by Machinist cybernetics. For he was Breed, and there was no telling how much of him was truly human, if anything at all. . .

He slid beneath the shelter of a brass panel and looked around, listening for the Guardsmen's footsteps with his unAugmented right ear. Their heavy armour meant that they were easy to pinpoint by the echoing clang of their boots. He

waited again, endlessly patient, till the nearest
had passed by, and then scampered closer to the
Pulse Hammer, ducking from cover to cover.

Somewhere, a particularly violent explosion
rocked the base. Chiro looked around the corner
of a small junction pod and located the control
panel, a wide swatch of steam-levers, press-studs
and switches, most of which were unmarked. The
corpse of the Chief Engineer was slumped across
it, his hand gone limp in the process of reaching
for the very thing that Chiro was intending to take.
The cortex key was a flat slide of translucent
spirit-stone, treated and etched to channel the
Flow that would power the machine. It was
intended to be a failsafe mechanism; in case
anything went wrong with the Pulse Hammer, it
could be removed and the Flow would disperse
uselessly. It was also a security measure against
just what had happened here.

They struck too fast, too unexpectedly for the
Chief Engineer to react in time and destroy the
cortex key. But these were just shock troops; they
had no knowledge of the workings of a Machinist
device. They had left the cortex key where it was.

That was an error of judgement.

He scrutinized the intermittent cover of the machinery between his position and the control panel. Dangerous. He couldn't see the patrolling Guardsmen anywhere, but was instead relying on their footfalls to guide him. He had no idea of their line of sight through the gaps between the banks of levers. Quickly, he tried to call up a plan map of the area in his head and marry that with the approximate location of the sentries to calculate their field of vision, but once again it was too complex for the pitifully inefficient synapses of his brain.

No choice. He'd have to chance it.

He dashed low and silent towards the control panel, flitting smoothly from cover to cover. His narrow shoulders were tensed in anticipation of a shout, and in his head he was already plotting alternative escape routes in case—

Then he was there. He pressed himself to the base of the control panel and waited, listening. The footsteps continued unabated. Stealthily, he reached up and around for the cortex key, guessing where it was on the panel above him. To

91

stand up would render him visible. He groped about and found it, slipping his fingers through the small metal grip on one end; but the angle was too sharp for him to draw it out of its slot. He shifted his position, raising his shoulder so that his arm could reach further round, and with an inward sigh of relief, he felt it sliding free.

"Hey! Who's over there?"

No time for regret or disappointment, just action. He pulled the cortex key the rest of the way free, sliding it into the deep inner breast pocket of his overalls, his mind already awhirl with possible avenues of progress, trying to calculate the one which combined the minimum risk of personal injury with the maximum chance of success.

"Don't fire at the machine!" the other Guardsman warned his companion urgently.

Ah, thought Chiro. An advantage.

"Come out from there!" came the harsh command. He could hear them prowling around, unable to see him. They would not fire on him to flush him out, but the moment he got clear of the Pulse Hammer they would take him. He was fast enough to avoid them, maybe; but with the cortex key on him, he could not take the chance of failure.

Swiftly, he tapped a sequence on the tiny studs set underneath the jawline of his mask. The first try produced no response; he reconsidered and entered a different sequence.

"Jikio," came the crackling reply. He was another Breed.

"This is Chiro. What is your location and status?"

"Secondary core. We are holding off the Jachyra for now, but the situation seems unlikely to continue in our favour."

"Request immediate and urgent shutdown of lighting facilities in the Pulse Hammer chamber and the surrounding chambers."

Jikio paused for a moment. "Understood," he said, and the line fizzled and cut to silence.

"I said come out!" shouted the Guardsman, his voice echoing around the chamber. "You think you can stay in there for ever? You're surrounded!"

Chiro tapped another stud, further along his metal jawline, and his vision recalibrated to a heat-sensitive setting. In the pitch darkness that was to come, it was more efficient than his low-light vision, which emulated the Kirin trick of making the most of even the tiniest amount of available light. This far underground, there would *be* no light, and the Citadel used not glowstones but bright, harsh sodium strips, powered by generators.

The room went black.

There was a cry of surprise from one Guardsman, a coarse oath by another. Chiro had already set his course and was running, heading for one of the three chamber exits. The cool surfaces of the idle machinery showed up a dark blue; where there was mechanical activity, the blue was a little lighter to reflect the increased warmth. Those bodies of the operators that he could see were still warmer than room temperature, but visibly darkening as he watched. He estimated ten seconds before the reserve lights kicked in. In that time, he had to—

The Guardsman was right in front of him, blocking his way to the exit, a bright, glowing smudge of greens, blues and yellows with a core of white at his heart. He was swiping around helplessly, panicked. Chiro's guess as to his location had been off; the acoustics of the chamber had confused his ears.

He could have evaded the Guardsman. He chose instead to forestall the chance of pursuit. Clenching his fist, he ran into the Guardsman and punched through his chest, his fist smashing through armour, flesh and bone and pulping organs on the way to emerging from the other side. The Guardsman was dead from shock long before Chiro braced his foot against the corpse's shoulder and pulled his hand free. A fast-spreading pool of green heat was oozing across the cool dark of the chamber floor as Chiro looked down on his enemy; then he ran, ignoring the other Guardsman's hollering for his companion.

Three seconds to go before he became visible again. He took two strides in preparation and then jumped, leaping to the roof of the corridor, grabbing a protruding handle. The access hatch that it was a part of swung down, returning his feet to the corridor floor.

Two seconds. He released the handle, jumped up again and smoothly pulled himself into the duct, sliding into the cradling womb of warm cables and pipes.

One second. He reached down and pulled the hatch shut.

The lights flickered back on as a secondary generator came on-line, throwing their illumination across the chamber again. There was a new corpse amid the multitude that were already there, this one wearing Guardsman's armour, a dark, ragged hole in its chest. The second Guardsman cast around the room frantically, searching for signs of the killer; but all else was stillness, and silence.

6

Some Part of Her Mind

{krel from antipole come carry newshe}

{?newshe come to hurt we?}
{agree, ?come to hurt we?}
{knownot}

{danger from newshe}
{?is danger?}

{newshe weak now}
{get stronger}
{danger}

{kill}

Mi'atte opened her eyes from the dream of hissing, whispered voices, blinked, and then remembered that her name was no longer Mi'atte. Kia, she was now. It didn't matter, really; one identity was as good as another, with no memories to back it up. Well, no coherent memories, anyway. Just the infuriatingly vague sensations that scratched at some door of her consciousness that she was unable to find.

The bed was too soft. She felt like she was perpetually on the verge of sinking into it, like quicksand. The white and silver silks were a startling and uncomfortable contrast to the hard, straw pallet she had slept on all of her remembered life. She looked around. The bed was in the corner of a small pavilion tent, the bright sunlight outside lightening the delicate purple fabric that surrounded her. A shielded lamp stood in a sculpted metal bracket stand near by, but no flame burned in it. There was a tall, free-standing mirror and embroidered screen in one corner of the tent, and a bowl of fruits and berries on a low, circular table next to the bed.

She remembered nothing of the journey from the mines, except fleeting sensations of biting cold and the rocking movement of something that carried them. Draining her stones to break free of the Overseer's power had exhausted her so much that she was unable to help drifting into a defenceless sleep. Her furs had been removed, but she was still wearing the grimy vest and trousers that had been her workclothes in the mines.

She slid her legs out from beneath the thin sheets and sat on the edge of the bed, took a spiky desert pear from the bowl on the table and began to peel it. Her tiredness had fallen from her sometime in the night, and she felt rested and refreshed. As she ate, she noticed a set of elegant white-and-blue silks that hung over the screen, that they presumably intended her to wear. She ignored them, finished her pear and got up. The sooner she found out what was going on, the better she would feel.

Someone wanted me to break out of there. Someone was helping me. They were helping me remember.

She walked across to the tent flap, ruffling her short, dirty red hair sleepily. What had the Overseer meant, saying that she was wanted by Macaan? Sure, she knew who Macaan was. The other mine workers talked about him enough, and his name was usually preceded by a string of insults. But *her*? What did he want with her?

Who was she, anyway?

She pulled aside the flap and squinted at the blinding desert sun that sliced in eagerly to heat her skin. Outside, amid the many-coloured tents that were pitched in an apparently random arrangement on the hard-baked dirt of the ground, the world moved on oblivious to her. Children played and ran, geckos flitted from shade to shade, people went back and forth with buckets of water or stood chatting in clusters. She guessed that she was in some sort of semi-permanent settlement; through a gap in the tents, she caught sight of some kind of perimeter fencing, a series of bulky, six-foot-high poles that bristled with Machinist equipment.

Desert-folk, she thought, observing their sun-darkened skin and airy clothing. *I'm in a nomad camp.*

A movement to her right caught her attention, and her eyes widened slightly in surprise as she saw what was approaching. Two krel, ten feet high at the shoulder, ridden by a man and a woman. She had never before seen the riding-beasts of the desert-folk, but she recognized them from the description that the miners had used when talking amongst themselves. They were repulsive to look at, their faces looking like something between horse and ape, with a dry, leathery beige skin that reminded Kia of Snappers. They –

(Snappers? Where did that *come from?)*

– walked on the knuckles of their disproportionately long and scrawny forearms, their heads hanging a foot or so beneath their high shoulder blades. A narrow body, lean and packed with taut muscle, tapered in a downward slope to thin hips and small back legs with wide, spatulate feet. The riders sat in saddles on their back, and they had reins and bits and bridles in the manner of horses.

They halted next to her and the krel obediently sat down, lowering their hindquarters so their riders could slip to the ground.

"You're awake, then," said the woman. "We were just coming to see you."

It was them, the pair from the mines that had rescued her. They introduced themselves as Li'ain and Jedda. Li'ain, the woman, was little older than Kia; she had smooth, beautiful features, but her blue eyes and odd accent revealed that she was not of the desert-folk, no matter what her deeply tanned skin might say. She wore tough, dusty travel gear, browns and greys, and her straight, lustrous black hair fell freely down her back and about her shoulders.

Jedda was perhaps past his twenty-fifth winter, with a slightly noble cast to his features that was offset by his mid-length, untrimmed hair. His skin was slightly darker than Li'ain's, and his eyes were deep brown. He spoke with the faint flattening and lengthening of vowels that was characteristic of the desert dialect, and his voice was soft and strong. He carried himself with a quiet confidence, and as their conversation went on, Kia noticed that he was not prone to any showy reaction or speech, but maintained a stable moderation in his manner.

"We left clean clothes for you in the tent," he said.

"I know," Kia replied. "Thank you."

"Shall we go inside?" he offered. "There is much we must discuss. Or would you like to bathe first?"

"No, thank you," she said, her voice small and a little meek. She was used to dealing with only two types of people; her fellow miners, and the Taskmasters. It was difficult to know how to react to these newcomers. She owed them gratitude, but mistrusted them at the same time.

"Then let us talk," Jedda said.

Kia retreated from the tent flap, out of the sun and back inside the warm pavilion tent. Jedda and Li'ain, leaving their krel outside, came in and joined her. There was a small wooden stool by the mirror; Li'ain took it and sat on it. Jedda remained standing. Kia returned to perch on the edge of the bed, looking from one to the other as if she were about to be interrogated or accused of something. Maybe she was.

"You have no need to be nervous," said Li'ain soothingly. "We did not help you escape from the mines only to hurt you now."

The reassurance did little to lessen Kia's trepidation. She took another desert pear from the nearby bowl and began to peel it, to prevent her hands from fidgeting.

"Why?" she said after a moment. She was unused to talking very much, and felt awkward doing it.

"Let us say for now that we are friends of *your* friends," Jedda replied with a smile. "And we would like to see the girl known as Kia brought back to us."

His reply only served to confuse her. "I don't remember Kia. She's just a name to me," she said. "*Was* that my name?"

"Yes," said Li'ain. "The Overseer named you Mi'atte only after he bought you, not knowing who you were. It means 'bargain' in the old desert-tongue."

"*Ei ju'ji ma'ta*," she replied softly. *I know what it means.*

"Ah, of course, you learned much of the

language of the tribes from the other miners, no doubt."

"I listened."

"Yet you still remember your native Dominion dialect."

Kia bit into the pear, the cool, sweet juices filling her mouth. She chewed a small piece and swallowed. "Did you know Kia?" she asked.

"Only by reputation," Li'ain said, leaning her elbows on her knees as she sat. "It was something of a famous name in Parakka, after the Integration."

"What did she do?" She had heard of Parakka, from the mines. After all, new people arrived every month, and they always brought news.

Li'ain laughed lightly, a high, chiming sound of merriment. "What did *you* do," she corrected. "Well, it depends on whose stories you listen to, but you are something of a war hero. Tales are told about your bravery and leadership at Parakka's assault on the Ley Warren, and later in the defence of Base Usido. And you are credited with recruiting the forces of the Koth Taraan on to the side of Parakka. Word spreads, you see."

Kia looked down at the groundsheet of the tent. "I don't recall her." After a moment, she looked up. "How did I forget? Why can't I remember?"

Li'ain and Jedda exchanged glances, but it was the latter who spoke. "It is thought that you were killed during the battle at Base Usido," he said, his words careful and sympathetic. "You, along with the Resonant girl Elani and a Kirin called Peliqua. You were all together when you were hit by a bolt from an Artillerist. If there were any remains, they were long lost to the fault that opened up beneath the area where it hit. For a time, people held on to the possibility that Elani had shifted all three of you to the Dominions a moment before the bolt struck. But when none of you returned, they were left no option but to believe you were dead." He paused, and smiled. "It seems that they were wrong."

"We do not know why you are unable to remember," Li'ain said, picking up the story with her lilting accent. "All that is known is that you were found, battered, in a shallow rock trench at the northern edges of the desert. Your wrist and leg were broken, and you were unconscious. It was . . . unfortunate that you were found by slavers, but perhaps you were lucky. The chances were against you being found at all."

"What about the others?" Kia asked. The names had sparked some kind of reaction inside her, but she could not pin it down. "Where are they?"

"There was no trace of the others," Li'ain said.

There was a silence for a time. Kia finished her pear, not meeting their gazes.

"We can help you remember, Kia," said Jedda. "There is a Da'al Jakai here in the camp."

"A healer," Li'ain supplied, seeing the look of incomprehension on Kia's face.

"Da'al Jakai," Kia repeated. It meant *sacrifice* in the ancient language of the desert-folk.

"It is your choice, Kia," said Jedda. "We are not your enemies. We will not force you to do anything."

Kia thought for a time. "Why are you doing this?" she asked. "Why are you helping me?"

"Because Parakka needs you," said Jedda. "And we, the desert-folk . . . we need Parakka."

"And because your brother thinks you are dead," Li'ain said softly.

Ryushi! The name came out of nowhere and hit her with an almost physical force. Her brother, her twin. *Ryushi!*

But his face, there for the most fleeting of moments, slipped away from her and she could not claw it back. All that was left was the pain of losing the memory. Well, no more of that. The old compulsion had returned with new strength, the need to remember that had burned in her ever since she was brought to the mines, the need to find this *Kia*.

"I'll do it," she said.

She floated, in a sea of cotton-wool nothingness.

Some part of her mind was watching her physical body from the other side of the tent, an invisible observer. Li'ain sat on her stool, intent; Jedda stood near by, concern etched on his brow. Before her was the Da'al Jakai, his huge hands laid together on top of her head as if in a blessing. She herself was asleep in a sitting position on the edge of the bed, dreaming, her eyes roving

beneath their lids and her mouth and fingertips
twitching occasionally.

{stronger she soon}

{?danger?}

{!much danger!}
{killkillkill}

{afraid hurtplace}

{!she hurtplace!}

The feeling was blissful, tranquil. The hissing
sussuration of voices that skated across the
surface of her unconscious were too faint to
distract her from the beautiful floating sensation.
She closed her eyes in her dream, and when she
opened them again the Da'al Jakai was there,
exactly as she had seen him in real life. Tall he
was, and narrow-shouldered, wearing a robe that
was comprised of uneven strips and slices of
many colours, but all of them somehow earthen
in tone, brown and russet and olive green. His

long black hair was braided and twined with strips and beads of the same colours, and his face was concealed behind an oval mask of white ceramic, with smears of coarse paint forming patterns across the cheeks and around the almond-shaped eye-sockets.

"Will you make me remember?" she asked.

"**Yes**," came the reply, an echo rising and fading before and after it.

"Will it hurt?"

"**Yes**."

"Because of what I will feel when I know who I was?"

"**Yes**."

"Can you make me remember without the pain?" she asked.

"**The memory and the pain are inseparable, Kia. We are defined by our suffering as much as our joy.**"

She did not feel afraid. In this place, it was impossible to feel fear. And so she closed her eyes and bowed her head, and let the Da'al Jakai place his hands amid the thatch of her red hair, as he had done minutes before in the real world.

110

{!beginning!}

                              {!killnow! weak she still}

              {cannot}

                    {?forget hurtplace?}

{she within hurtplace}

                    {then hurtplace destroy we}

She frowned momentarily as the voices intruded once more into the tranquillity of her dream-state, but in the next instant they were forgotten as she felt a great warmth, and then she and the Da'al Jakai seemed to flow together, becoming liquid, mixing into each other, and for a time she lost herself. . .

It was a moment of clarity and understanding, in which she saw everything. The Da'al Jakai, the bearers of the sun-yellow spirit-stones, those who were called *sacrifice*. They were the healers, the people who had the power to take on others' wounds. A man's broken leg could be cured only if the healer's own broke in empathy. A woman's madness could be salved only at the expense of the healer's own sanity. For an injury could not be cured instantly, not by any force in the universe; it could only be transferred.

But the spirit-stones that the Da'al Jakai bore also accelerated their own healing, physical and mental, to many times that of a normal person. The Da'al Jakai took on the pain of others and then healed themselves, and the one whose mind twined with Kia's now would become amnesiac for a time after he had completed his task of restoring her memory.

She saw everything about the man who now, delicately, deconstructed the walls that had been built up around her. She saw the horror on his parents' faces as the spirit-stones they had bought for their infant's *pah'nu'kah* turned yellow in the Deliverer's hand. She saw the crying child, only ten winters old, as the tall, many-coloured men arrived to take him away, take him to their monastery in the arid rock outcrops of the southern deserts, where he could be schooled in how to use his power without killing himself accidentally. The calm, the inner peace of seclusion, were all revealed to Kia in that instant; the meditative trance that had to be attained in order to cleanse the impurities that they took into themselves from others.

She felt an unravelling around her, threads of thought and feeling coming free, and something terrible approaching, something *awful*. . .

Her eyes flicked open, and she screamed, a terrible sound of grief and misery that seemed to last for ever. The Da'al Jakai stepped back, ignoring the alarmed stares of Li'ain and Jedda, and bowed his masked head.

"What have you *done*?" Li'ain cried.

"The pain of her memory is great," came the reply. "That, I cannot bear for her."

Jedda, unable to stand by and watch, hurried over to sit next to her, and offered a comforting arm around Kia's shoulders. She turned her face into his chest and screamed again, the noise muffled by his silk shirt and his body, and he gathered her closer and held her while she wept and raged.

"Walk with me," said the Da'al Jakai to Li'ain. She looked at Kia, reluctant to leave, but Jedda motioned with his head that she should go.

"I will watch over her," he said.

Li'ain went with the Da'al Jakai out of the tent, into the furious light of the sun. People who had gathered in curiosity at the howling coming from within dispersed unobtrusively as they emerged. As she passed, she brushed an absent hand across the muzzle of one of the two krel who squatted where they had been left, grunting and snuffling.

"What was it?" she asked the tall figure that walked slowly with her.

"She has lost much. First her mother, then her father and family. Then her elder brother, who is now her hated enemy. Then her *twin*, from whom she has become alienated, and to whom she spoke her last words in anger before they parted over a year ago. Now she has lost her partner, and for that one she has had no time to mourn. She has remembered them all now. The shock is great, but it will ease quickly. I have done all I can to aid her recovery."

Li'ain looked down at their shadows on the dusty ground and brushed her long, dark hair back behind her ear. "Does she know what happened? Why she lost her memory?"

"Now she does," came the reply from the mask. "Her mind had blanked it out. I was forced to remove the memory entirely, or it would stay festering inside her, like a cancer; but I left her with the knowledge of what happened, if not the recollection. She knows where she went, but she can remember nothing about it."

Li'ain tilted her head up at him, waiting for an explanation.

"The Resonant girl Elani did indeed shift them during the explosion that many thought had killed them. But she was a fraction of a second too late. They absorbed a portion of the initial shockwave of the blast that killed Kia's loved one. Elani's shift was interrupted; she was knocked unconscious during the transference. There is no telling what the consequences of that might have been. However, for Kia, the result was perhaps more favourable than she had a right to hope. She made it to the Dominions. But on the way, for the most minute of instants, she was exposed to that which only the eyes of the Deliverers may see. Netherfane."

"I know of Netherfane," Li'ain replied.

"It exists between the two worlds. Resonants cross it when they shift, but a subconscious instinct prevents them from ever entering it. Due to the interruption, Kia was witness to it somehow. The moment was small enough to cause her mind to blank itself, unable to cope with what it saw. She entered the Dominions in the wrong place, fifteen feet from the ground, and fell to the rock floor below. Her memory began from the moment when she woke up." He paused. "I have removed the cause of the problem; and now her memory is restored. All except for the sight of Netherfane; that I had to remove and take for my own. She must rest for a time."

"Thank you, Da'al Jakai," said Li'ain, coming to a halt. The taller man halted with her. "But what of her companions?"

"She remembers nothing of their fates. It is reasonable to assume that they, too, have made it to the Dominions; but where they entered this realm and whether they survived the entrance is another matter. Kia appeared fifteen feet above the ground. It could as easily have been fifteen feet *below*."

116

Li'ain was silent, her face grave.

"I must go now," said the Da'al Jakai. "Already I feel the onset of the blankness I have taken on. The madness of witnessing Netherfane is sure to follow."

Li'ain looked up into the eyes of the mask, chilled by the casual tone with which he spoke of such horrors. "Thank you," she said again, and this time there was more than just the gratitude for what he had done for Kia, but also for what he had done for *her*.

"Many atonements must be made before this age is done," said the Da'al Jakai slowly, catching the subtext in her words and sensing what it meant. "I pray for yours."

That was when the Sa'arin attack began.

7

Coming Home

The bright sun of the Dominions beat down on the yellow leaves of the nanka trees, brightening the forest bowl and dispelling the shadows of the surrounding mountains. Beneath the canopy, shaded somewhat by the gently stirring fingers of the foliage, Gar Jenna waited anxiously. It had grown and thrived since the Integration, doubling in size in the two years since Macaan had defeated the forces of Parakka at the Ley Warren; now its carefully constructed wooden walkways, huts and buildings spread almost the whole way down the opposing canyon walls, reaching towards the rushing river at the bottom. The stout rope bridges that spanned the chasm from one side to the other had multiplied, low arcs like clothes-lines between the two halves of the settlement. Dwellings occupied every fold and plane of the canyon now, the coarse red-yellow of the rock submerged beneath the darker colour of nanka wood.

Gar Jenna, the first stronghold of the Parakkan forces, had never been found by Macaan. Though the entire army of Parakka had attempted their desperate assault on the Ley Warren, there were many who were not fighters who had stayed behind. The Machinists, the artisans, the pregnant or sick or injured, the young, the old; though many in Parakka were warriors, as many again were not. Parakka did not believe in forcing its members to fight, and still others who were willing were ordered to stay rather than throw their lives away needlessly.

When word had reached them that the Parakkan army had been annihilated without trace, there had been despair and grief. But after the mourning, life went on. As Macaan tightened his grip on the Dominions, more and more people were in need of sanctuary. Those who were left behind at Gar Jenna went out to gather the disillusioned, the oppressed, the ones who were willing to fight back. They were not short of choice. And so Gar Jenna began to swell again, and Parakka began to rebuild itself, to regenerate.

Then, just over a year ago, *she* had come. Elani, the little Resonant girl, like a messiah of hope; and with her, members of the new Parakkan force, that had thrived in the darkness of Kirin Taq. They explained how the army had not been destroyed but displaced, and how they had grown in secret, not daring to send Resonants over to their fellows in the Dominions for fear of alerting Macaan's Jachyra. But now Macaan knew of their presence, they had made contact at last. Relatives and loved ones thought long dead were revealed to be alive; but the dire plight of the Parakkans in Kirin Taq dampened the celebrations a little.

Those in Gar Jenna could do little to help. Instead, they were told to bide their time, to grow, to wait. If Parakka survived in Kirin Taq, then one day they would be coming back to the Dominions. Elani had left, returning with the troops to the warzone, and the denizens of Gar Jenna had heard nothing, hoping and hoping for the day when they would return.

That day had arrived at last, but this time Elani was not with them, having disappeared in the battle at Base Usido a year before, soon after leaving Gar Jenna.

The artificial canopy of leaves began to draw back to welcome the morning. Pulleys and cranks whined as the immense camouflage netting slowly receded, its ragged shade retreating down one side of the canyon wall, across the river and up the far side, driven back by the bright sunlight. The water came alive with white sparkles, and the shadows cowered into cracks in the rock. Somewhere, a lookout shouted.

And there they were, dark, winged silhouettes dropping out of the dazzling orb in the sky, forty or more. A flight of wyverns, screeching as they descended. The long-separated Parakkans from Kirin Taq were coming home.

Ryushi's chest was bursting with a searing joy as he glided down through the trees to be swallowed up by the canyon. The sun on his face was a delight he had longed for ever since the Integration, and to see Gar Jenna again – his first place of sanctuary after the massacre of his family – heartened him more than he could say. Araceil sensed his happiness and shared it, as they gently descended through the webwork of rope bridges towards the massive landing-platform at the base of the canyon, a steel structure that spanned the river beneath them.

The canyon walls were lined with cheering people, leaning against the wooden railings of the walkways and waving as the multitude of wyverns carefully made their descent, swooping slowly down like tumbling black-and-white leaves. The noise around them was deafening, swamping them.

"I'd never thought I'd find my way back here," Calica said, seated in the harness behind him. Ryushi looked over his shoulder, smiled and reached back to squeeze her hand in his.

"And this time . . ." he said. "This time, we're winning."

She returned the smile and then looked hastily away before the embarrassed flush at his touch could overtake her. She had been gone for so long, so much wasted time during which she had only been able to see Ryushi sporadically. When they had met, they had been distant. She, denied her freedom until she had deactivated the heartstone; he, caught up with his new Bond-wyvern, sharing a level of understanding with the creature that she could not hope to attain with him. She knew how he had been driven to Bond out of despair and loneliness, and she blamed herself for not being there for him. But her mission had been more important than her personal feelings.

She looked over at where Hochi guided another wyvern down, with Gerdi clinging to his belt. The big man's face was grim, even amidst the celebrations; Gerdi seemed a little subdued in his presence. Hochi's black moods had grown increasingly common of late. His obsession with deciphering some kind of hidden meaning in Tochaa's pendant had spiralled out of control over recent months; and with the pendant's mysterious disappearance, taken from around his neck as he slept, he had lapsed into a period of dark brooding. Even Gerdi knew better than to try and cajole him out of it.

There would be celebrations tonight, but as Calica watched Hochi steer his wyvern with expert fingers, she guessed that he would not be at them.

The longhouse was alive with music and laughter.

Situated on a wide semicircular platform that fanned out of a flat section of the canyon wall, the longhouse had originally been the great communal hall for Gar Jenna, where meals and conferences were held. Now that Gar Jenna had expanded, new and larger eating-houses had been constructed; but it was felt curiously appropriate that the focal point of the celebrations should be the old longhouse that the new arrivals knew so well.

The atmosphere of unrestrained merriment was infectious, and spread far beyond the immediate party. As the night fell and the leaf canopy was once more drawn over Gar Jenna, the darkness became a sparkling net of orange stars, a thousand windows lit up by glowstone-light. The return of the lost Parakkans meant more than a homecoming, more than the reunification of broken families and friendships. It was the first tangible sign that the tide had turned, that Parakka were no longer on the run from Macaan. They had liberated Kirin Taq, an entire continent. Now they were back to reclaim their homeland.

Ryushi leaned against the railing of a walkway that stood a little way distant from the longhouse, joined to it by a set of stairs that jutted from the rock of the canyon wall. The noise of the celebrants seemed to drift and echo in the great gulf of the chasm, spreading out into the cool night air. Beneath him was an abyss, studded with orange lights, and he looked over it and felt a faint smile come to his lips.

"Know something I don't?" said Calica from behind him.

"I might have guessed *you'd* find me," he observed good-naturedly. "How'd you get me this time? Your stones?"

"No," she said, leaning on the railing next to him. "I followed you out."

"Sneak. I must be slipping; should've seen you."

"Hey, don't forget I was doing this whole Parakka thing years before *you* were," Calica said, swiping him on the arm. "I might just have picked up a trick or two."

125

"So what's up?"

"Oh, this and that," she said evasively. "So what were you smiling about, anyway?"

"Can't I *smile* now?" Ryushi asked in mock-exasperation.

"Not without telling me why," she said. "I've missed being in on your secrets over the last year."

Her tone was playful, but there was a seriousness in what she said.

"I know," he replied. "I've missed having you hassle me, too."

"*Hassle* you? You're making me sound like Gerdi!" she protested.

"S'only a joke," he said, turning his face slightly towards her. Framed by long, matted locks of hair, his smooth elfin features and blue eyes bore few of the scars that he had sustained in the service of Parakka. It was as if his partnership with Araceil had revitalized him, made him shine again, even after the tragic loss of his twin and Elani. He seemed strangely content now, more at ease with himself. Happy, even.

Calica twirled a lock of her orange-gold hair

absently as she leaned her elbows against the stout wooden railing, looking out across the darkened canyon. For a time, they did not speak. Finally, it was she who broke the silence.

"It's been a hard year for me, Ryushi. I had a lot of . . . responsibility put on me. More than I was used to," she said, hesitantly.

"It's okay, Calica. Nobody should have to carry the kind of burden you did."

"No, it's *not* okay," she said, sounding a little angry at herself. "I mean . . . with all that had happened to you. . . I was your friend, I *am* your friend, but . . . I should have been there for you. Everyone left you, just when you needed them, and I was the worst."

"I'm alright, aren't I?" Ryushi said. "I made it through. Don't beat yourself up about it."

She looked at him, and in her eyes was a mild scepticism. "I'd like to believe you," she said.

"Calica, it's *okay*," he repeated, sliding his arm around her and hugging her. For a moment, she was too surprised to respond; then she relaxed into him, a pleasurable glow spreading through her body. "You're still my friend," he said.

He released her, and she drew back almost guiltily. She hadn't meant to let her guard down like that. She still did not trust herself enough, not after so long away from him, not when she knew that she was still in love. And not when she still did not know how he felt about her. It was too cruel, that he should have left Base Usido with Whist the very day that she had been about to overcome her stubborn pride and tell him how she felt, and then to hear the rumours that the Princess Aurin had won him instead. And when they finally did meet, the heartstone and Kia's death combined to keep them apart. A year spent suffering the frustration of not being able to complete what she had begun, always fearing that Ryushi was slipping away from her, always wondering who was on his mind: her, or her Splitling Aurin?

"You weren't at the Council meeting," she said after a time, changing the subject to avoid discomfort.

Ryushi half-shrugged. "I figured you guys would get along fine without me."

She laughed; it was another joke. Ryushi had

never shown any desire to be on the Council, and he was not a particularly suitable candidate anyway. That had been Kia's end of things. "I meant, you weren't in the *audience*," she said, conceding him the point.

"I had a vision," he replied, putting the first three fingers of his right hand on his forehead and affecting an expression of deep concentration. "I saw . . . us two standing on a balcony . . . you telling me everything that happened. . ."

"Will you *stop*?" she cried, laughing again. Now he was gently making fun of her own powers of premonition. He certainly did seem lighter of heart than she had ever remembered him.

"Okay, okay," he said, grinning. "So tell me, what's the news?"

She watched him with amused suspicion for a time, in case he was going to say anything else. He put on an innocent face.

"Alright," she said. "It's the usual mix of good and bad. The Keriags deserted the Dominions and Kirin Taq as soon as I got the heartstone, a year or so ago; they went back to the Ley Warrens and stayed there. They weren't interested in fighting

Macaan, and they didn't dare kill him anyway while the heartstone existed. They just wanted to be left alone. Anyway, that decimated Macaan's forces. He responded immediately by bringing in a series of conscription measures, by increasing the penalty for even minor crimes, and by calling in every one of his Guardsmen to the cities to maintain the illusion that he was still in power. He stamped on the people before they could rise up."

"Conscription?" Ryushi asked. "I thought he already had just about every blue-stoned manchild in the land for his Guardsmen."

"Well, now he's taking everyone. Any manchild above fifteen winters has been called in for a mandatory three years active service, stones or no stones. And the sick thing is, most families even welcomed the idea, because it means that their children get to be fed properly."

"Food's running out?"

"Macaan has never paid much attention to agricultural policy," Calica replied. "He takes the lion's share for his own men."

"That's no way to rule. It's just asking for a revolt," Ryushi said thoughtfully.

"That's the thing," she said. "Since he lost the Keriags, since we let him believe he lost Aurin" – here she glanced at Ryushi, to see if he reacted at her name; he didn't – "he's got . . . careless. Everything seems to be done with no regard for the future. I mean, he's conscripted almost two-thirds of the male population already, which is pretty much everyone who's fighting fit. Apart from slowing the economy down massively, that also leaves him with one big problem."

"In three years' time, when their service is up, he's got no army," Ryushi finished.

"Worse," Calica replied. "He's got thousands of trained soldiers who he'll have to return to the poverty they left behind. He's practically creating an army to revolt against him."

"So what's he up to? You're the tactician."

Calica drummed her fingers on the wooden railing. "I have no idea. It looks like he's going all or nothing. Maybe he only wants to beat us. Or it could be a smokescreen, I don't know." She paused, then slapped her palms on the railing in frustration. "If we had been able to attack a year ago, we'd have swept him off the land. But it's too late now; he's dug in. It's going to be much harder to get him out, and we're going to be fighting against our own people."

"Can't we turn them around? Get them on our side?"

"Maybe," said Calica. "Maybe."

They stood in silence for a time, the still canyon air resounding with the sounds of merriment.

"The Nomen on the eastern steppes are still free," Calica said suddenly. "But they've never bothered with mainland politics, and Macaan's left them alone so far. He's making a push south into the deserts, but we don't know why. He's spreading himself. It seems to run counter to his tactic of consolidation. And he's invaded the Machinist's Citadel."

"What? Why?" Ryushi exclaimed.

Calica gave him a look. "*I* should know? It was only a matter of time, anyway. Why pay for what you can take?"

"I thought it was pretty much impenetrable," Ryushi mused.

"So did the Machinists, evidently."

A pause.

"I'm going in to find out," she said.

"To the Citadel?" Ryushi asked in surprise. "It's that important?"

"The Citadel is the biggest repository of technology and weaponry in the Dominions. Who knows what they've got in there? If Macaan's going for a tactical advantage, we have to know what it is."

"But why you?" Ryushi asked.

"Because I volunteered. It's *okay*," she said, lightly patting his cheek, "don't worry, Hochi and Gerdi are going with me."

"I hope you know that we're coming too," he said. The *we* referred to him and Araceil.

"I kinda thought you'd say that," Calica replied, and inside she was smiling.

Ryushi straightened and flexed the taut muscles of his back. "I haven't hit anything really *hard* in far too long," he said, then offered a hand to Calica. "Come on, there's a party going on that we're missing."

8

The Last Precious Thing

The chambers of the Master Machinist, Okre Jey, were wide and low, dark and dimly lit by flickering striplights. The walls, floor and ceiling were tarnished metal, cold and somehow greasy. The air hummed with the internal workings of the Citadel. The room was so spartan that it could easily have been mistaken for unused warehouse space, with only a few coiled-iron chairs and a heavy terminal desk swarming with meters and dials and press-studs.

Okre Jey himself was more machine than man, ancient and bent, his frail human body buried beneath a mass of cables, strips of metal exoskeleton, utility pods and life-support equipment. His face was a narrow alloy mask, with blank, bulbous lenses for eyes and a thick, trunk-like cable that ran from his mouthpiece to a respirator pack on his chest. He wore a ragged beige shawl that hung over his shoulders and hunched back to the floor.

The Master Machinist cared nothing for comfort. His eyes had long since failed, and he had refused to allow new ones to be installed. There was very little left of his nervous system near his skin for him to feel sensations with. But his brain was as keen as it always had been, and his knowledge of technology was unparalleled; he had been the director of the Machinists for many winters now (twenty-seven years, eight months, seven days, ten hours, forty-three minutes and nineteen seconds, by his internal chronometer) and so, when Macaan had a demand to make of his newly conquered prisoners, it was Okre Jey that he came to see.

Four Jachyra stood around him, on guard, as the heavy door to his chambers hissed open in a cloud of steam. Macaan stood there, his face lowered and shadowed in the feeble light, his arms hidden inside the folds of his long purple-blue cloak.

"Old man," he said, his voice thick with menace as he walked across the room towards the Master Machinist. As he reached them, he grabbed the pipe that ran to Okre Jey's respirator and pulled the masked face up to meet his own. His usually serene features were twisted in anger, and his androgynous beauty had been corrupted by a snarl. "*Where* is the cortex key?" he roared.

The Jachyra shuffled uneasily.

"*You appear to have mislaid it, my liege,*" came the reply, the voice flattened and distorted by the artificial larynx that translated the vibrations of the Master Machinist's throat and tongue into recognizable sound.

Macaan threw his prisoner down and stalked away a few paces before whirling back to point at him. "Be aware, old man, that I am playing no games now. I will tear this place apart to find it, and I will execute as many of your people as is necessary to get what I want."

"*The Pulse Hammer is not yet fully tested and operational. We removed the cortex key to prevent you inadvertently harming yourself.*"

Macaan's eyes blazed, and he looked for a moment as if he would strike the Master Machinist; but suddenly he cooled, reverting to his customary calm, and it seemed as if a different person had suddenly stepped into his body and taken control.

"I see you mean to show the appropriate amount of rebellious spirit before you are ready to listen," he said. "Shall we skip the formalities, old man? I would rather not waste the time."

"My liege, as you may be aware, I do not have the cortex key that will render the Pulse Hammer operational," said Okre Jey, his glassy lenses staring at nothing.

"Are you not in contact with the one who has it?" Macaan asked.

"I am in contact only with the highest echelons of Machinist society. They pass on the information I need to know. Otherwise I would be privy to thousands of questions and demands every day." He paused, tilting his head upward. *"My liege saw fit to render inactive the greater proportion of my contacts. You are wasteful and inefficient."*

"I am also the King of this realm," Macaan

137

sighed. "So wasteful or not, I still hold the power of life or death over everyone in the Dominions. Including you and your people. Now I know that it was taken by a Breed named Chiro; we accounted for every member of the Pulse Hammer staff on duty except for that one. What I want, is for you to tell him to surrender."

"He will not. He is Breed. Breed are grown in vats, without human parents, and brought up to serve a specific purpose. They aspire to think like machines. He will follow his last order, even if you threatened to execute every Machinist, one by one. If he was told to take the key and keep it safe, that is what he will do."

"Unless either the person who gave him that order or a superior Machinist tells him otherwise," Macaan finished. "Unfortunately, we do not know who gave him that order."

"You have broadcast an order already from my closest subordinate," Okre Jey said. *"It did no good."*

"That's right," said Macaan. "Which leaves me with one possibility: it was *you* who gave the order."

138

"Unfeasible. I am not in contact with any Breed."

Macaan leaned in close to the Master Machinist's earpiece. "Well *someone* did it," he whispered, then straightened suddenly. "It doesn't matter," he said. "He will not refuse an order from you."

"You are correct," said Okre Jey. *"Therefore, you leave me only one option."*

Macaan stepped back. "And what is that?"

Okre Jey did not reply. Instead, he jerked once, and there was a soft hiss from somewhere beneath his dirty shawl. His body seemed to become boneless, and he slumped in a crumpled heap on the floor, thin wisps of smoke rising from his body.

Macaan blinked. The Master Machinist's suicide – or rather, his *self-destruct* – could scarcely have been less ostentatious and for a moment the King was not sure what had happened. After a time, he sniffed dismissively and tossed his long, white hair.

"Take that out of here," he said. "You know what to do. Vore, you stay."

+++ **Yes, my King** +++

The other Jachyra picked up the corpse and left, their unnatural joints making their movement jerky and odd. Vore regarded the King warily. He stood uncommonly straight for a Jachyra, a full seven feet in height, with his disproportionately long arms ending in particularly outsize claws. His eyes were replaced by a single band of red, and his speaking-grille had been shaped creatively into a downturned mouth. Macaan stood with his head bowed, one finger curled across his chin in thought, and waited for the door to hiss shut behind him.

"I'm disappointed in you, Vore," he said at length.

+++ **Yes, my King** +++ came the tinny reply from the Jachyra's mouthpiece.

"It was a careless slip, to allow even one person through your net. It may cost us dearly, if this Chiro decides to destroy the cortex key. Assuming that he hasn't already."

+++ **I agree, my King. But as you may recall, my Jachyra and I were occupied with attacking the power cores; the Pulse Hammer and its**

surrounding chambers were the responsibility of the Guardsmen that we brought through with us +++

"That is so, Vore. But as my new Chief of Jachyra, I expect better from you. Tatterdemalion would have ensured that no such thing could happen."

+++ My King, Tatterdemalion is dead. He failed +++

"Vore," the King said softly. "You take too many liberties. I am not accustomed to my subjects arguing with me. Have a care, Jachyra, and be glad that I am a reasonable man."

The Jachyra's reaction was unreadable beneath the metal and rags that mummified him. **+++ My most humble apologies, my King +++** he said, bowing. The motion was disturbing to the eye; he bent to a right-angle at the waist and then straightened.

Macaan studied his new Chief critically. He had never been entirely happy with his new choice; Vore had always had a tendency to overstep his bounds, and the respect he gave his King seemed disconcertingly false at times. There had been many times that Macaan had been tempted simply to kill him with a thought, to use the indigo trigger-stone in his forehead to crack the stone that was implanted deep in Vore's body. But he had come to see it as a test of restraint, a way to gauge his own stability. After all, he had been tempted to kill *all* of his closest aides at one time or another over the last year. The trigger-stone made it pitifully easy to do.

But he held himself back. Because there were times now when he was not quite . . . rational. Times when he would do things that the cold light of reason would reveal to be foolish. He had to watch himself these days, in case the rages that came upon him would destroy his carefully laid plans.

Daughter, he thought. *Aurin. They killed you. The last precious thing I had.*

He closed his eyes, squeezing them tight, oblivious to the creature that watched him.

Now there is only vengeance.

9

Every Last Piece

The desert had literally come alive.

The nomad camp where Kia had been taken stood on a gravelly flat at the foot of a sizeable rock outcrop. The ground there was more stony than the soft, yielding sand of the desert, but not so hard that it was impossible to drive the disruptor posts into it. The posts formed a wide, three-quarter circle around the thick knot of brightly coloured tents, with the last quarter facing up against the bulk of the outcrop. High dunes shouldered nearby, shielding the camp from the horizon.

But the sand was moving. The Sa'arin were coming.

They moved like something out of a slow-motion nightmare, cresting and breaking like waves. Half-formed, vaguely humanoid shapes, they rose out of the sand with distorted faces that shifted and melted, two simple eyes and a mouth made of hollows and shadows. Their thick arms ended in clublike, fingerless fists, and they seemed to be swimming through the dunes, rarely surfacing above their waists but rising to eight feet high even then. They shed sand constantly from their huge bodies, giving them a curiously shaggy appearance, and they groaned and wailed at the sky as they came, the noise horribly mournful.

The Sa'arin. The word meant *sand-ghouls*. They were creatures made of the living desert, the ancient spirits of the sand. And they were angry.

"What is it?" cried Jedda, rushing out of the tent where Kia lay. The Da'al Jakai had gone, disappearing into the depths of the camp. "The Sa'arin? Now?"

Li'ain scanned the camp, one hand on the reins of her krel to calm it. "Something seems to have stirred them up," she said. "I will go and see."

Jedda laid a hand on her arm. "You stay with Kia. *I* will go and see."

Li'ain held his gaze for a moment. She knew well the meaning behind the words. *You aren't of the desert-folk, you don't know how to handle this.* A flicker of frustration ignited in her; she had lived in the desert almost two seasons now, winter and spring (such as they were), and weathered four Sa'arin assaults in various camps. But she would never be accepted as one of them, even by a friend like Jedda.

She looked down and away. Well, let him be like that. She had Kia now; she would be gone from this place soon, maybe never to return.

Am I not good *enough for them?* she thought bitterly, and walked past him into the tent, not caring if he saw her anger. He let her go; he knew better than to try and salve the hurt he had unwittingly caused. Instead, he offered his waiting mount an absent pat and then headed for the perimeter, drawing his scimitar. The two krel, realizing that their services would not be needed for a while, grunted and folded their long forelegs underneath them, settling down to rest.

Inside the purple-hued shade of the tent, Kia lay curled up in a foetal position on the bed, her face buried in the crooks of her elbows. Her screaming had stopped, but her body still shook violently with sobs. Li'ain regarded her for a moment. This girl, in whom she had invested so much time and hope; was she really all that her reputation made her out to be?

For a time, she stood awkwardly, not knowing what to do. Human contact was not something she had been brought up with, and dealing with extremes of emotion disconcerted her. But it took only a short while for her unease to be overcome by a greater discomfort; she could not stand by and watch such distress without trying to offer some consolation.

And so, tentatively, she crossed the tent and sat down next to Kia, just by her head. After a moment's hesitation, she laid her hand on the girl's shoulder. Kia broke into fresh tears at her sympathetic touch, and Li'ain drew back in mild alarm; but then Kia moved, laying her head in Li'ain's lap as if she were her mother, even though there was perhaps a single winter between them. Again, a short period of uncertainty, a fear of doing the wrong thing . . . and then Li'ain laid her hand again on Kia's side, the other one stroking her unwashed thatch of red hair, comforting her like a child.

It wasn't so hard.

The tortured groans and howls of the Sa'arin clashed with the pulsing hum of the disruptor posts as Jedda ran up next to another desert warrior and looked out across the dunes.

"There's so many," the other man muttered, his arms folded.

"I do not like it," said Jedda, his sword still drawn and ready. Ten or twenty metres away from them, just beyond the disruptor posts, the Sa'arin were rising up as if against some invisible barrier, moaning and then crumbling only to rise again. The cacophony was horrendous. "Their numbers are far greater than before. They do not shy away from the perimeter, but throw themselves on to it. They have a purpose."

He looked to the left and right. Men were arriving in force now, crowding around the edges of the camp, but most still had their weapons sheathed. They watched the Sa'arin as they might

147

watch a furious creature in a cage; warily, but safe in the knowledge that it could not reach them. Yet between them, there were no bars, only air. It was *beneath* the ground that the barrier held.

The disruptor posts were one of the few Machinist inventions that the desert-folk had adopted into common use. In their long-running war against the Sa'arin, the devices were the single most useful weapon in their arsenal. They put out a disruption field under the surface of the sand, agitating the tiny grains many times a second. The Sa'arin, who not only moved through the sand but were actually *made* of it, found it extremely difficult to pass these fields. The effect, Jedda imagined, was like having their bodies shaken to pieces. It did not kill them – nothing *killed* them, as far as they could tell – but it provided the first truly effective defence against their assaults.

It was not unheard of, however, for the disruptor posts to fail. And Jedda did not share the confidence of his fellows when he saw the rabid vigour with which the Sa'arin were flinging themselves against the field.

* * *

"I lost Ty," Kia whispered hoarsely, her sobs quietened now, the side of her head pressed into Li'ain's lap. "I lost everything. Everything I ever had, every last piece of my life. My home, my friends, my family. All because of him."

"You mean King Macaan," Li'ain said, smoothing Kia's hair.

"Macaan," she repeated. "Yes, King Macaan."

"You still have your brother," Li'ain said.

"He could be dead, for all I know," Kia replied, her voice empty of expression, her face tear-streaked.

"Oh, no, he is still very much alive."

There was a pause.

"Who *are* you, Li'ain. Did Parakka send you?"

A short laugh. "Parakka think you are dead. So do their enemies. It is best that it should stay that way for now."

"So who are you? You're not of the desert-folk."

"I'm a friend," she replied.

"That's not an answer," Kia said, without any force in her tone. "What do you-—"

{hurthurthurt}

{hate}

{newshe}

{no time}

{huuuurt}

{must hurt to kill}

{kill newshe}

{must}

{hate}

{now}

Kia sat up suddenly in alarm, her grief overwhelmed by the new emotion.

"What is it?" Li'ain asked, alert.

"The things outside," Kia breathed, listening to the noise that filtered through the purple fabric of the tent. "What's attacking this place?"

"Sa'arin," Li'ain replied. "Sand-ghouls. It is all

right, we are safe while they are outside the perimeter."

Kia scrambled off the bed and to her feet.

"They're coming in."

A cry went up from further along the perimeter, and Jedda was seized by a sudden and sickening lurch of fear as he set off at a sprint to investigate. For a few seconds, his view was impeded by the corner of a white pavilion tent; but then he came into sight of the disturbance, and he realized that his doubts about the disruptor posts had been justified.

The Sa'arin were piling themselves against the disruption field, throwing their bodies at it relentlessly, two of them crowding up for every one that shivered apart. By their very nature, they could not exist when out of contact with the sand; that was why the disruptor posts spread their fields beneath the surface, why they could not simply step over it. So they were slumping into it instead, washing into the perimeter like waves faster than it could tear them apart.

Making a battering-ram with their bodies.

"Keep them out!" Jedda barked, but it was

useless. As he watched, the creatures hammered past the disruptor posts, bursting through the invisible dam in an avalanche of sand. To either side, the disruptor posts blew out in a shower of sparks, overloaded by the sheer weight of the attack.

The Sa'arin were inside.

"Warriors! To me!" Jedda cried, his sword raised high as he roared the command, and ran in to attack.

For those who were directly behind the section where the disruptor posts had failed, there was little hope. The wave of sand that burst through had not even slid flat before the looming, shifting shapes of the Sa'arin were rising out of it, their club-fists raised high like maces, bringing them smashing down among the desert-folk with deadly force. Their monotonous, death-like groans reached a new pitch as they bludgeoned their way inward, riding on the momentum of their initial assault, driving through the defenders.

Jedda was the first to arrive of those who ran to repel the invasion, swinging his scimitar to hack through the arm of one of the creatures as it swept its hollow eyes around, looking for fresh victims. The creature wailed mournfully and collapsed in a cascade of sand, but the disappearance of that one only revealed another Sa'arin behind it, sweeping a slow, massive hand down at him. He dodged aside, and the fist slammed into the stony ground in a shower of stinging grit. With a cry, he buried his curved blade into the sand-ghoul's shoulder, and it burst apart like its companion, the force that held it together dispelled.

Steel. That was all it took. Piercing the creatures with metal somehow interfered with the controlling energy and caused them to break apart. Jedda did not understand the physics of it, only that it worked. Sa'arin attacks never lasted long; they had only a finite amount of power with which to keep creating new bodies. Experience had taught the desert-folk that the more sand-ghouls they destroyed, the more had to be replaced, and the faster the attack ended. It was just a matter of holding back the tide till then.

{hurtplace gone}

{kill newshe}

{kill newshe}

{kill}

"Shut *up!*" Kia cried as she hurried out of the tent, looking around as if to find the source of the grating, whispering voices.

"Kia!" Li'ain called, following her out. "Where are you going?"

"Can *you* hear them?" Kia asked, still casting about anxiously. The krel were back upright again, faintly alarmed by the commotion. Now they dipped their long, horse-ape faces to watch the two humans.

"The Sa'arin? Of course I can," Li'ain replied. The moans of the attacking creatures were all about them.

"Can you hear the *voices*? What they're *saying*?" Kia persisted.

Li'ain regarded her with an expression of mingled amazement and hope. "You can really *hear* them? I never thought. . ."

"Li'ain, I don't have the time," Kia replied impatiently. The tears on her face had not even dried, but she had forgotten them for the moment. "It's *me* they're talking about. They're after *me*!"

"Wait!" Li'ain called, but Kia was already away, running towards the sound of nearby conflict. She cursed and followed, drawing a long, slender blade from the scabbard at her belt.

The fighting around the breach in the perimeter had spread further into the camp. The defenders simply did not have the numbers to hold back the encroaching Sa'arin; and now that the creatures were inside, they were able to emerge from the ground at any point in the settlement. The attempt at repelling them was scattered and undisciplined, as people ran to protect their loved ones instead of concentrating on specific combat goals. They were being steadily whittled away by the creatures, havoc erupting throughout the bright tents.

Jedda's face ran with salty sweat under the

blazing sun, as he side-stepped a thundering blow to bury the wicked edge of his sword into a sand-ghoul's chest. Several men were fighting with him now, battling the Sa'arin at the point where they had penetrated the perimeter. There was no particular tactical sense to it – the Sa'arin had already slipped past them, invisibly, beneath the ground – but it was as good as any other place in which to face the creatures. The faster they destroyed their enemy, the faster the attack would end and they could repair the disruptor posts.

A loud groan from behind them prompted one of the defenders – a young, dark-skinned hothead named Jin – to look around at the source of the sound. He cried out in anger as he saw a sand-ghoul rising out of the ground to swing a fist into the side of a long tent of soft blue, collapsing it. *His* tent, where he had left his betrothed, asleep, when he had left that morning. It proceeded to pound the remains of the tent, pulverizing everything inside.

"*Kili!*" Jin cried as he turned from the battle to attack the new foe, his face set in rage.

But the distraction had provided one of the other Sa'arin with the opportunity it needed. A great arm of sand swung down towards him with a force that could crack bones. . .

. . .and met the edge of Jedda's scimitar. The Sa'arin turned to a heap of loose sand at the touch of his blade, spraying Jin with a hard shower of grains. Jedda, taking advantage of a momentary lull, grabbed Jin's arm roughly.

"She is *there*, you fool," he said, pointing with his weapon towards where a tall, slight girl was fighting with the rest of the menfolk. "Go to her side, if you cannot keep your mind on your own survival."

"I obey, *Rai'kel*," Jin replied, and ran off to join her.

Kia and Li'ain had left their tent not a moment too soon. They were only a few dozen metres away, heading for where Jedda fought at the perimeter, when the purple folds suddenly seemed to crumple inward. Six of the Sa'arin creatures formed around it at the same moment, smashing at it viciously from all sides, like someone trying to kill a mouse under a rug.

Li'ain looked back at Kia, who gave her a glance as if to say: *See?*

"They really *are* after you! Why?"

157

"I don't—" Kia began, but her words dissolved into a surprised yelp as the ground before her suddenly bulged upwards, and another Sa'arin rose up, its long, distended face like a child's sketch of a ghost. Sloughing off sand on all sides, it towered eight feet above them, even slouched as it was. It gave off a great, dreary howl, and almost immediately Kia felt the ground behind and to all sides of them begin to respond, as more of its companions arrived.

{newshe!}

{newshe!}

{newshe!}

{found newshe}

{kill}

{kill}

{before she hurt we}

{hurt we}

{kill she}

{kill}

"Uh-uh, guys," said Kia under her breath. "*Don't* think so."

The power in her spirit-stones jumped at her call, eager to be summoned after being so long dormant. Like a jolt, it slammed through her, and with a cry she dropped to one knee and slapped her open palm on the ground with a resounding *boom.* A shockwave raced outwards in a circle from the the epicentre, a great subterranean pulse, sweeping all before it. Those Sa'arin nearest her dissipated immediately; it took a few seconds to reach those on the edge of the camp. Where the shockwave hit the sand-ghouls, they turned to loose sand. On the surface, a thick ripple caused tents to buckle and knocked men and women and krel from their feet; but beneath the surface, the force was much greater.

In a moment, it was over. The camp was in disarray. Several of the disruptor posts leaned at odd angles. Kia stood, the only one not to have been unbalanced by the blast. People began to pick themselves up off the floor slowly, looking around in alarm and amazement.

Silence had fallen.

10

Of Passive Resistance

"This is gonna be rough!" Ryushi shouted over his shoulder to Calica. "Hang on!"

He had hardly finished his sentence before the first force-bolt seared through the air beneath them, and Araceil swooped right as the formation of wyverns scattered. Calica held on to the sides of his belt, pressed against his back in the rear seat of the harness. Both of them lay low against Araceil's spine at an angle so that Calica's chin was just above Ryushi's middle back, their legs strapped securely against the creature's flanks.

Riding a wyvern was not like riding a horse or a pakpak; apart from the fact that a wyvern's body was too broad to sit comfortably astride, the wind resistance at high speeds would tear a person out of their harness if they were upright when flying.

The harnesses were constructed to put their riders in a position that was half kneeling, half lying on their bellies, with their shoulders slightly raised by padded pommels. Calica was glad of it now, for even as one who had flown several times before, the acceleration of a bull wyvern like Araceil still made her heart flutter.

Before and below them, made small by perspective, was the dark cone of the Machinists' Citadel, sitting on its immense crag with the dark, moist green of the fens and valleys spreading around it. The landscape bore little evidence of the recent battle that had resulted in its occupation; the hulks of the destroyed war machines had been cleared away, and only the occasional section of bracken that had been blown flat by a force-bolt or crushed under the tracks of some vehicle testified to what had passed.

It was a false serenity. The first thing Macaan had done upon occupying the Citadel was lace the fens with traps, set patrols of both Guardsmen and Jachyra, and utilize every Machinist device he could lay his hands on to make the Citadel unapproachable from the ground. Parakka had learned as much from those few who had lived in the area and escaped Macaan's attentions long enough to make their way east.

There were nineteen Parakkan wyverns in all, three flights of six and one extra. All of them, with the exception of the last, were Bonded to their riders. This was a special assignment that required manoeuvrability above all else, and a Bonded rider was almost always a superior flyer to one that was not. It was only natural; to share the thoughts and instincts of their mounts afforded them a great advantage.

The last wyvern, the only one that did not belong to a flight, was piloted by Hochi. Behind him in the harness sat Gerdi, and behind him was Quain, a Parakkan Machinist.

The first force-bolt from the guns of the Citadel was the signal for the rest of the artillery to open up, and the sky suddenly filled with the almost invisible pulse of force-cannon fire. Ripples of displaced air tore through the wheeling paths of the wyverns, but at this distance the bombardment was ineffective, and the riders dodged easily. The trial would come when they began to close in on their target.

Ryushi kept his eyes on his flight leader, Jikkio, who was some way ahead of him. She was easily recognizable by the stream of black hair that flowed out behind her.

"You think this is gonna work?" Calica shouted over the din.

"I've gone with slimmer chances," Ryushi replied, sparing her a wry glance over his shoulder. "Not many, though."

"You really know how to tell a girl what she wants to hear," Calica called back.

"Ah, come on, this is a cakewalk," he grinned, and up ahead Jikkio raised her hand to give the signal, and Araceil plunged into a stomach-lurching dive.

The movement was beautifully synchronized. The nineteen wyverns had been performing random, evasive swirls as they approached, making it hard for the guns to track their erratic movements; now, as one, they suddenly plummeted towards the ground, dropping at a terrifying speed towards the flat moor beneath them.

Calica was gripping Ryushi's belt hard enough
to hurt him as the yellow-green splashes of ferns
and grass raced towards them like a wall. The
guns had lost them completely for the moment,
but this did not even occur to her at the time. She
was concentrating on quelling the fear that
threatened to well up into a scream.

Pull up, pull up, pull UP!

And then, when it seemed that it was far too
late to avoid collision, Araceil shifted his
forewings and braked with his immense hind
wings, levelling out a mere ten feet or so above
the ground. Calica felt her body strain with the G-
force of the manoeuvre, and her head went light;
but Araceil, Bonded as he was to a human, had
intentionally eased the movement just enough to
avoid causing unconsciousness.

She shook her head, coming out of the
momentary disorientation, and looked around
them. They were tearing along the moor at
breakneck speed, the carpet of muted colours
beneath them smudged into an unrecognizable
mass. The other wyverns were to either side of
them; she spotted Hochi some way off, a little

higher than the others. Gerdi looked faintly green.

"Some fun, huh?" Ryushi beamed, and Calica wanted to hit him.

It was a good plan. The wyverns were to approach high in the sky, to allow the automatic targeting systems of the Citadel's guns to lock on to them. Then, as soon as they got close enough for the barrage to become dangerous, they dropped as hard and fast as they could to near ground level. The force-cannons would lose their lock, and it would take time to search the area and re-acquire them. By that time, the wyverns hoped to be close enough to take advantage of the valleys and crags that surrounded the Citadel, putting themselves beneath the range of the guns.

Greater minds than theirs had thought of similar plans, but it had one major flaw; to attack the Citadel, the wyverns still had to get high enough to get an angle on the immense construction, and that meant being in the firing line of the guns. Landing for a ground assault was pointless, because they would have to fight their way up through the treacherous passes of the valleys, putting themselves at a great disadvantage.

However, that particular flaw was of no concern to Parakka. They didn't intend to attack the Citadel. They just wanted to get close to it.

"You okay back there?" Ryushi enquired. His belt was being held so tight that he was getting pins and needles in his thighs.

"Just fly," Calica replied nervously, glancing at the rushing ground beneath them. Araceil's trailing feet were low enough to knock someone's head off if they should pass over them.

"Not far to go," he said. "We'll be safe from the guns as soon as we hit the valleys. They're not gonna get us now!"

A moment later, a force-bolt shrieked out of nowhere and smashed into the ground behind one of the leaders, sending up a rain of fist-sized chunks of earth.

"You've *got* to learn to shut up," Calica said.

"Where's your sense of comic timing?" Ryushi replied, banking Araceil hard left and right to avoid another bolt that destroyed a section of ground just ahead. Racing towards them was the jagged, uneven lip of a valley, eating up the moor as it approached. The guns picked up in earnest now, but their attack had come too late. They only managed another six shots between all nineteen of the wyverns before the canyon lip finally slid under the intruders and they dropped into it, swooping languidly down into its protective cradle.

The valleys were relatively wide, carpeted with grass and the occasional herd of goats that roamed on sides so steep that it seemed impossible they should keep their balance. The defensive fortifications down here were all ancient and rarely manned; they saw evidence of old bunkers and ratchet-operated bolt guns such as had not been seen in the Dominions for fifty years. Nobody worked them now. The guns of the Citadel had stopped. Silence fell, except for the heavy *swoosh* of the wyverns' wings.

They had expected perhaps a little resistance from the King's wyverns, even though their intelligence had indicated that he had sent a large fleet to aid his generals in the southern deserts; but either he had drained his air fleet completely or they were not coming out. It was almost peaceful, as they glided through the dark green of the valleys.

Ryushi looked over at Hochi, and pointed down to a sheltered cave at the foot of a wide section of shale, surrounded by thick bracken. Hochi looked back at Quain for approval; Quain nodded.

"Down we go," Ryushi said, and he and Hochi slid downward, out of formation, towards the valley floor. Jikkio raised a hand in salute to both of them before the remainder of the flight was carried out of sight. A few moments later, they heard the guns start up again.

The mission was essentially a decoy. The wyverns would appear to be scouting, on a reconnaissance mission for Parakka. After they came out of the valley, they would circle the Citadel at a reasonably safe distance for a time, drawing the fire of the force-cannons while staying out of effective range, before departing again. Nobody would notice that they were two short when they left. If they did, they might assume that they had been shot down or crashed.

Not worth making a great search effort for, anyway; certainly not when Macaan was having troubles of his own inside.

Quain had been a Machinist in the Citadel for many years before defecting to Parakka. He assured them that the Machinists would not take kindly to having their Citadel occupied. They would, most likely, be operating a system of passive resistance: "accidentally" overlooking vital maintenance on machinery, "forgetting" to re-prime the pressure cores and so on. If they could get into the Citadel, within range of the transmitters that most Machinists carried, then they might find they had a lot of people on the inside willing to help them out. Of course, first they had to get there. And Quain had an idea about that.

Ryushi and Hochi put their wyverns down in the patch of bracken outside the cave mouth and unstrapped themselves from their harnesses. Araceil did not scent anything inside, except the moist smell of mould and faint decay, so they judged it was a safe place for the wyverns to wait while they carried out their mission. Araceil dipped his great, boxy muzzle down to Ryushi's level, and Ryushi roughly patted the skull-mask of bone armour that surrounded his head.

"See ya later, Araceil," he murmured. Calica watched the two of them with what she was surprised to find was a faint jealousy.

Araceil urged the other wyvern – who, being unBonded, did not share the same understanding – into the darkness of the cave, leaving the five humans outside.

"Okay, Quain. Your show," said Calica. "Where are we?"

All eyes turned to the Machinist. He was a slight man of fifty or sixty winters, with one side of his face and head Augmented and one side flesh. The flesh side was gaunt and grizzled with stubble, with thin white hair across his scalp; the Augmented side was covered in tiny devices that clicked and chattered, reminding Ryushi of Corm. He wore the standard single-breasted black greatcoat and high collar of the Machinists. There were many younger Machinists in Parakka, but few who claimed to know the inside of the Citadel like Quain did.

"This way," he said, his voice deep and phlegmy despite his small frame. "We'd best be out of sight in case Macaan sends anyone lookin'."

They deferred to him in his own territory, and wordlessly set off after him through the knee-high foliage, occasionally glancing up at the sky or along the valley walls to check for signs that they had been detected. Hochi's face was hard. Gerdi seemed uncharacteristically quiet, but that was probably a blessing under the circumstances.

"So what exactly is this place that you're taking us to to?" Calica asked. It was an unnecessary question; she had already been told during the briefing at Gar Jenna. She just wanted to hear Quain talk, to get the measure of him a little more. And with Hochi and Gerdi so evidently strained, and her own feelings about Ryushi worrying at her, he was the easiest target for a conversation.

"The old south-eastern mine shaft," Quain replied. "It's long been covered over, but if this Ryushi boy does what he says he can do, it shouldn't be a problem gettin' in."

"And Macaan doesn't know about it, right?" Ryushi put in, kicking aside a tough knot of bracken.

"Oh, he prob'ly *knows* about it," Quain said, waving a hand absently in the air. "But he won't be concernin' himself with it. It's as secure as any of the doors into the Citadel. Never needed guards before, prob'ly won't waste 'em now."

"But you can get in?" Ryushi asked.

"I *tole* you I could," Quain replied. "Wouldn't have come all out here otherwise. 'Sides, coming in through the mines is the best way to not get seen. Nothin' down there but the ur-Lan."

"Oh."

They made their way hurriedly along the valley, hugging the sides to obtain what cover they could. Overhead, the sound of the guns had dwindled to a few stray shots; the Parakkan wyverns had obviously finished their decoy.

"There it is," Quain said, suddenly pointing. At a place where the grass gave way to a sheer patch of rock, a rectangular portal sat at ground level. Enormous pillars of wood supported a vast crossbeam, almost as grey with dust and age as the stone around it. Rubble was piled up between the pillars, with mildew and moss that had gathered over the years seeming to cement it together.

Ryushi considered it for a moment, his weight resting on one leg. "There's no quiet way to do this, is there?" he asked rhetorically.

Calica answered him anyway. "Just blast it, quickly," she said, glancing up at the sky again. "The guns are still firing the odd shot. Time it so it sounds like a force-bolt impact."

"Stand back," Ryushi said, although they were all still some distance away. He lowered his head, closing his eyes in concentration, and bunched a fist. A steady hum began to build around him, the sound of his spirit-stone batteries gorging on Flow energy from the earth. Carefully he gathered it, storing it, waiting. . .

Somewhere above, a gun punched out another force-bolt.

Ryushi threw his arm out straight and a pulse of energy fired from his shoulder and out from his fist, warping the air around its invisible body as it streaked into the rubble blockade and hit it with a dull *wham*. The rubble blasted apart, pulverized, exploding outwards and inwards as if detonated, belching out a thick cloud of dust. The spray of pebbles ricocheted all around Ryushi, held off by his bubble of energy defence.

When the dust cleared, a section of the rubble had been destroyed, and the rocks above it had slumped down to fill its place. A wide gap, high up in the rock pile, had been opened.

Calica laid a hand on his shoulder. "You were pretty restrained that time, Ryushi. That's not like you. Usually you'd have taken half the valley with it."

Ryushi shrugged and made a noise of indifference. "Maybe I've mellowed in my old age," he replied.

"Don't even *talk* to me about old age," Quain grumbled as he walked past them towards the mine entrance.

It was a tricky task to clamber through the gap on the bed of newly disturbed rocks, but Ryushi pointed out that the hole he had made was a lot harder to see than if he had cleared the entire blockage, and could even be mistaken for natural subsidence if nobody looked too closely. Hochi grunted as he squeezed his great bulk through last; Gerdi didn't say a word about it. That, if anything, was more disconcerting to Calica than his silence. He never missed a chance to provoke Hochi about his weight. What was going *on* with those two? Had the mysterious loss of Tochaa's pendant made Hochi *that* unapproachable, even for a boy who was practically his son?

Inside the entrance, the darkness was absolute. Only the narrow, driving needles of sunlight from outside pushed back the shadows a little way, catching the softly drifting motes of dust that had been stirred up by Ryushi's assault.

"You got the glowstone, Gerdi?" Calica asked. The young Noman boy obediently pulled out the stone from his pack and unwrapped the rag from around it. A soft orange light spilled out in all directions, illuminating the rocky tunnel that they stood in. Wooden support beams, struts and angle-joists marched away a short distance to where a wide metal elevator waited, sheening dully. It was a simple cage, with mesh on all sides strengthened by iron bars and a rusty metal floor.

"Will this thing still work?" Hochi asked, eyeing it dubiously.

Calica gave him a momentary look, a little surprised that he had spoken.

"Should think so," Quain replied, studying the descent/ascent mechanism through the grille of the elevator roof. "It's only been out of use five winters or so."

"Five winters," Ryushi repeated flatly.

Quain harrumphed. "Without maintenance, something like this'll still be operative after *twenty* winters. Just might stick, is all."

"What if it doesn't work?" Hochi asked, his warhammer slung over his shoulder.

"There's an emergency ladder. But it's a long climb down. *I'm* goin' in the elevator."

Ryushi consoled himself with the fact that he could probably shield them if the lift cable snapped, but it did little to quell his unease as he stepped into the elevator with the others. There was a long, tortuous creak from above.

"Don't worry," Quain said. "'s just loosening up."

Calica laughed nervously.

The elevator took them down after a few heart-stopping jolts at the beginning, which Quain assured them was simply the mechanism "workin' off the rust", and soon they were descending relatively smoothly down the shaft. The orange light of the glowstones slid uncomfortably over the dark rock walls that pressed in on them, the shadows retreating as they approached and then growing again as they passed. The air felt damp and tasted of mould.

The descent was not a long one – Quain told them that the mines were close to the surface – and it was less than three minutes before the elevator clattered to a noisy halt at the bottom of the shaft. Another short tunnel led to a large trapezoid metal gateway, wider at the base. The gate was a solid slab of metal, studded with circuit panels, sensors, and other barely identifiable devices.

Quain ushered Gerdi closer, and walked over to a panel to the right of the gate where a horizontal row of six small brass dials sat on the left of a rectangular palm-stud. Muttering to himself, he turned each one to the appropriate number and then slapped the palm-stud at the end.

Nothing happened.

"Hmm," Quain said.

"That better not mean what I think it means," Gerdi said, holding the glowstone up to the older man's face.

"Hmm," Quain repeated, rubbing his hand across his face thoughtfully. "I never thought they'd get round to changin' the code."

"You didn't, huh?" Gerdi asked blandly, then suddenly shouted at him: "So *now* what are we supposed to do?"

"It's okay, Gerdi," Calica said calmly, walking up from behind. "You think I hadn't thought of that? Give me *some* credit."

Quain and Gerdi made space for her at the row of dials, the Noman boy shooting poisonous looks at the old Machinist. Calica took a breath, and then closed her eyes, gripping the first dial between the pad of her thumb and the side of her index finger. The hum of spirit-stone energy built up around her, quieter and more subtle than Ryushi's. For a few moments, she was still. Then, slowly, she turned the dial till she was satisfied with its position. In silence, the others watched while she repeated the cycle all the way along the row. Then she opened her eyes.

"There!" she smiled, and hit the palm-stud.

There was a rumble from somewhere deep in the rock, a distant clank, and then the gate began to slide upwards into its sheath. Beyond was a cavernous rock tunnel, faintly lit by glowstones high above, strewn with rubble and the occasional piece of rusted mining equipment. It was cold and still, and bore the signs of long disuse. The sound of the opening gate echoed off down the tunnel, as if eager to fill the dead air.

"All is as it should be," said Quain confidently. "Come on!" He went off through the gate, without waiting to see if they would follow. Ryushi and Gerdi exchanged glances that said: *who brought him?*

They walked down the tunnel for a way, picking their way carefully over the chunks of rock and old piping that lay about: Quain in the lead; Calica, Ryushi and Gerdi behind him; and Hochi as self-appointed rearguard.

"So how'd you pull that trick with the door, Cal?" Gerdi asked. He seemed brighter and more animated with Hochi trailing behind.

"It's easy enough," she said. "The dials remember. The amount of times they've been put in the correct sequence is far more than the times when people have got it wrong. So I figured that had to be the right combination."

Gerdi whistled. Calica had been improving on her psychometry – the ability to see past events connected with objects she touched – just as Ryushi had been honing his own skills. Her talent had been erratic before; it was much more reliable now.

Reliable enough to get into Ryushi's head? she thought. It had been over a year since she had tried to see into his mind in the same way she had seen into Macaan's just before the Integration. Maybe she could do it now. Maybe she was afraid that she'd find Aurin there.

She shook off the thought as she noticed the growing lights and the repetitive sparking of cannon rams up ahead. Quain walked blithely onwards down the centre of the tunnel, and they followed his lead towards the great archway that rose up before them. As they stepped through, the rock walls fell away, and there before them were the Machinist mines.

Well, they might have got into the Citadel okay,
but will they ever get out again? And is Quain
all that he seems to be?

There's only one way to find out. . .

Read

Broken Sky

Part Eight

Or you'll never know . . .

Remember these classic Broken Sky moments?

Ryushi blasting the golem. . .
"Okay," he said quietly. "Enough."

The first appearance of a Jachyra. . .
*The stranger's fingers spread wide, and with a
sudden* shrik, *sharp metal nails appeared.*

The Deliverer performing a pah'nu'kah. . .
*Deliverers were shrouded in mystery,
surrounded by legend.*

The arrival of Elani. . .
*"I want you to look after her. She's a very
special girl."*

Tatterdemalion reporting back to the King. . .
"A few Resonants still elude us."

Calica fearing for the future. . .
*"Macaan is building up to something.
Something terrible."*

Hochi paying Gerdi back for stealing the pastries. . .
"I'll make a pastry from your head*!"*

**You won't if you haven't read Parts 1–6.
How can you bear it?**

Walkinstown Branch Tel. 4558159